GRIZZLY

'CAUTIONARY TALES FOR LOVERS OF...

D0829236

FREAKS OF NATURE

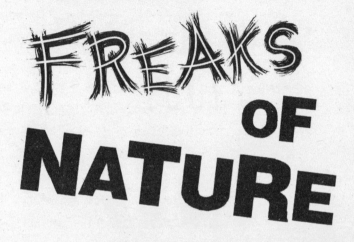

WARNING!

THIS BOOK IS PROTECTED BY ANTI-DEATH GLUE
THE PAGES OF THIS BOOK HAVE BEEN SUPER-GLUED
TOGETHER TO PREVENT OPENING. DO NOT OPEN
OR YOU WILL BE IN IMMEDIATE DANGER OF DEATH.

YOU THINK YOU'RE SO HARD, DON'T YOU?

Also in this series:

GRIZZLY TALES

'CAUTIONARY TALES FOR LOVERS OF SQUEAM'

FREAKS OF NATURE

JAMIE RIX

Illustrated by Steven Pattison

Orion
Children's Books

THERE ARE VERY BAD THINGS BEHIND THIS DOOR. THEY MEAN TO DO YOU HARM.

IF YOU PASS THROUGH THIS DOOR INTO THE DARKNESS IT WILL BE YOUR FUNERAL!

For Jack the BEng

First published in Great Britain in 2007
by Orion Children's Books
a division of the Orion Publishing Group Ltd
Orion House
5 Upper St Martin's Lane
London WC2H 9EA

3 5 7 9 10 8 6 4

Copyright © Jamie Rix 2007
Illustrations copyright © Steven Pattison 2007

The rights of Jamie Rix and Steven Pattison to be identified as the author
and illustrator of this work respectively have been asserted.

A catalogue record for this book is available from the British Library.

Printed in Great Britain

ISBN 978 1 84255 552 1

Only those people with no eyes to see, no fingers to feel, no nose to smell, no ears to hear and no brain to imagine can safely pass beyond this point. All other people who wish to proceed into THE HOTHELL DARKNESS should wear protective clothing.

RECOMMENDED LIST OF PROTECTIVE CLOTHING

BROWN WATERPROOF TROUSERS*

Wear at all times in case of unforeseen accidents of the 'I'm so scared I couldn't help myself' variety.

*Now available in a variety of colours – brown, brown, brown, brown, brown, brown and brown.

HORROR HAIR NET*

Tidies away straggly curls to prevent Freaks of Nature leaping off the page, grabbing your hair and dragging you into the book.

*Virtually invisible except when you're looking at it.

A SLEEVELESS JUMPER

Saves losing the sleeves to your favourite jumper when Freaks of Nature rip off your arms at the shoulders.

BUTCHER'S APRON

Prevents nasty blood stains on sleeveless jumper.

ICE HOCKEY MASK

Obstructs Freaks of Nature from inserting straws up your nostrils and sucking out your brains.

VEST

Keeps you warm in winter.

All items are currently available from the Death by Book Clothing range

(www.deathbybookclothingrange/grizzlyprotection/buynowbeforeitstoo

lateandyougetkilledhorribly.com)

WELCOME TO

THE HOTHELL DARKNESS

BREAKFAST 7.30AM - 9.30AM.

NO MAN-EATING PLANTS UNLESS BY PRIOR
ARRANGEMENT WITH THE MAN.
CONGRATULATIONS! YOU ARE OUR SIX-BILLIONTH
GUEST. PLEASE ACCEPT A COMPLIMENTARY BOTTLE
OF CHAMPAIN (SPECIALLY FERMENTED TO GIVE YOU A
SPLITTING HEADACHE) AND A FREE MEAL IN OUR
AWARD-WINNING RESTAURANT, 'BODIES'. OUR MOTTO
AT THE HOTHELL DARKNESS IS, 'NOTHING GIVES US
MORE PLEASURE THAT TO SERVE OUR GUESTS!' AND
ONCE THEY HAVE BEEN SERVED, NOTHING GIVES US
MORE PLEASURE THAN TO WATCH OUR OTHER GUESTS
EAT THEM.

TONIGHT'S CHEF'S SPECIALS
COCKY ST JACK
LEGS BENEDICT
POOR HELENE

The Night-night Porter

7

Before I can show you to your room I must ask you to complete a short questionnaire. There's no mistake. All rooms in the Hothell Darkness are booked automatically when you are born. We monitor your behaviour as you grow up, then at the first sign of badness we open the curtains, turn down the sheets and put a chocolate on the pillow.

Of course you're BAD. You're a CHILD, aren't you? This ruler says you're one of the BADDEST children in this hothell. If you don't believe me put your nose on the page and measure it.

CRUELLER RULER

...that bad, really
A bit rotten round the edges
Bad bones
VIP Guest at the Hothell Darkness
Evil as a stink fish

2 3 4 5 6 7 8 9

See. You're as evil as a stink fish. And if that doesn't qualify you for your own room, I'm a fairy's tutu. Which in case you're wondering, I'm not!

I'll show you how bad you really are Answer these five questions TRUTHFULLY.

Do you prefer your peas in pods or telephone boxes?

What is the ideal number of legs you think a spider should have? 2. 3. 4 or 8?

When bottle-brushing a bush baby

Actually. I can't be bothered. Who cares whether you're bad or not? I've locked the door now so you're not going anywhere. You're ALL MINE! FOREVER!

Don't be dismayed. There's plenty to do down here in the Darkness. You could help pass eternity by doing our twenty-billion-piece jigsaw of the inside of a black hole or by reading our Visitor's Book. It contains the stories of some of our 'honoured' guests, which is why I call it *The Book of Grizzly Tales* because it's a book of tales, and the children in the tales come to a grizzly end! Have a peek! Feast your greedy eyeballs . . . while you've still got them!

The wicked children in these stories thought they'd take on MOTHER NATURE. but, as you'll find out, she's not the sort of mother you take on! She's the sort of mother who chases you round the room with a coal shovel and blackens the seat of your pants. She's the sort of mother who poisons your drinking water and fills up your school rucksack with stones!

I wish she was my mother . . . God love her!

Help! I'm on fire!

I don't want to be useful!

Does anyone know what the time is?

I'm not c...c...c...cold!

Don't string me up!
Leave my lid on!

They're just six of the billions of children who live in the Hothell Darkness, thanking me for making their stay so pleasant. You'll meet them later.

Now. Nature is a funny old stick. Did you know, for example, that bats hang upside-down, because if they stood upright their legs would snap? And it's not because they've got really thin legs. It's because I've got metal traps set on all their

perching places. Nature is full of INTERESTING
FACTS like that. which I shall be sharing with you
as we go along.

INTERESTING FACTS ABOUT NATURE

Number 36 – Exploding Ants

All ants will explode as long as they are stupid
enough to stand out in the sun under the heat of a
magnifying glass without asking a few basic
questions, like: 'What am I doing here?', 'Why
am I getting hotter and hotter?' and 'Why is my
belly blowing up like a lilo?' It is because ants
never ask these questions that the hot air inside
their abdomens can expand unchecked until its
only way out is to explode through the ant's body
armour with such force that it splatters the
ant across nearby blades of grass like a
teaspoon of spilt caviar.

As all good tales do. this first one starts with
exploding ants. Of course what these particular
exploding ants in this particular story were NOT
aware of was that a larger force was at work

The Night Night Porter

FRANK EINSTEIN'S MONSTER

The boy's name was Frank Einstein. With a name like Einstein you might have expected him to be rather clever, but you'd be wrong. He was the type of boy who laughed when he exploded ants underneath his magnifying glass, and roared with glee when a fat one burned. As it exploded, hundreds of pieces of flaming formic-flesh shot across the grass and set fire to the lawn. Frank had never seen anything so pretty as those licking flames. In fact, had it not been for his quick thinking mother who extinguished the flames with a bucket of water Frank might never have seen anything ever again.

'Frank!' she cried. 'Look out! There's fire in your eyes!' Actually, the fire was in his eyebrows, so low had he stooped to peer at the blazing grass. His eyeballs were seconds away from meltdown when the water hit his face.

But this was the day that Frank discovered fire. From then on he became obsessed with it. He lived for the noise of a striking match, for the orange flare as the head burst into life, for the crackle of the fire's greedy fingers, for the smell of its smoky breath, and for the relentless march of its flaming foot soldiers as they destroyed everything in their path. Fire seemed to satisfy the megalomaniac in Frank. Hiding behind a bush as the fire engine tore down the street to extinguish the empty rabbit hutch on the allotments; the reeling out of the big hose, the whoosh of the high-pressured water. It was very exciting and Frank took pride in the fact that *he alone* had made it happen.

For the next five days he lit fires all over the village and got away with it. He burned cardboard boxes in the supermarket car park, piles of rubbish in back yards and stacks of old tyres on the wasteland by the pond. But on the sixth day he was caught red-handed. Having dropped a match into a postbox, he got his wrist caught in the slit and a policeman had to pull him free.

'I don't understand what you think you're doing,' said Sergeant Douser, when Frank was shoved in front of the duty desk at the local police station. 'Why would anyone in their right mind set fire to letters in a postbox?'

'I was sending them by hotmail,' sniggered Frank.

Sergeant Douser had been around the block a few times. He knew how to deal with cheeky children. 'I've seen wasters like you before,' he said, leaning across the counter and dragging the boy towards him. 'Nothing is as dangerous as fire. Got it?'

'What about a tiger with its tail on fire? That's got fire *and* a tiger so that would be way more dangerous, don't you think?'

The policeman dropped Frank back on the floor.

'Anyway, fire's not dangerous. I wouldn't play with it if I thought it was.'

'You do know that fire breathes the same stuff as us to stay alive?' said Sergeant Douser. 'And there's only so much oxygen to go around.'

'I'm not stupid,' said Frank.

'Then answer me this. Imagine you start a fire in a small room with no windows. Who's going to breathe the oxygen first – you or the flames?'

'Me!' said the boy without hesitation.

The policeman shook his head. 'The

fire can be everywhere at the same time. It will reach inside your lungs and steal every last drop of oxygen it can find!'

When Frank said nothing Sergeant Douser thought that he had finally made his point, but Frank was just not listening.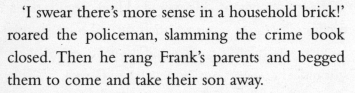

'You have to admit though,' he said suddenly, 'it *is* pretty. Fire, I mean.'

'I swear there's more sense in a household brick!' roared the policeman, slamming the crime book closed. Then he rang Frank's parents and begged them to come and take their son away.

I'd have had him put down. Well, it's kinder in the long run. Sadly, policemen don't have these powers any more.

* * *

Frank's parents laid down the law. They told him that his fire-raising had to stop before somebody got hurt, but at school the following day he set fire to his food.

'What are you doing?!' yelled the terrified dinner lady.

'This curry's not hot enough,' he sniggered. He was suspended indefinitely. When he got home his parents confiscated every match they could find and locked him in his bedroom.

'You can come out when you've learned to behave like a sensible human being!' said his father.

But Frank had other ideas. Unbeknownst to his parents, he had a secret stash of matches hidden under his floorboards and he let himself out by burning down his bedroom door.

His poor parents despaired. How could their firebrand of a son be stopped? It turned out that the answer was right in front of their eyes, on the smouldering bedroom door, charred black by the smoke and flames. Two words had been scratched into the soot:

FIRE LORD.

When they Googled the name they found a website, which contained a short message: 'The Fire Lord cures all fire-related disorders – permanently!' The word 'permanently' was flashing to draw attention to it. Then, under the heading 'Contact Me' were the following instructions: 'Send Smoke Signal and I shall arrive hot foot.'

As luck would have it, the ashes from the bedroom door were still smoking and Mr and Mrs

Einstein had to do nothing more than open and close the window six times in order to let out six clouds of smoke. Ten minutes later the air throbbed with a guttural roar as a chrome-encrusted Hot Rod car screeched to a halt outside the house and the Fire Lord stepped out.

He introduced himself to Mr and Mrs Einstein with a warm handshake and explained that his real name was Gooseberry. Lord Gooseberry.

He's a good friend of mine.

Frank's parents smiled politely at this stranger, whose bright-red skin and hairless body (apart from the triangular black beard on his chin) made him shine like a polished billiard ball.

'Hot spots to you,' he said. 'Is the patient around?'

'I'm afraid not,' said Mrs Einstein. 'He ran off after he burned down his door.'

'Expellent!' cried Lord Gooseberry. 'I want to discuss his secret cure.' While he'd been speaking he had written something down on a piece of paper. Now he tore the paper off the pad and handed it to Mrs Einstein. 'This is the answer.'

'Does that say "fire"?'

'My goodnose yes! *Fight Fire with Fire!*' he s.
pulling out his collar to let a cloud of steam escape
from inside his shirt. 'Is it just me or is it hot in
here?'

'Just you, I think,' said Mr Einstein.

'Then best get on before I melt. Young Frank's
cure of a permanent nature is to allow him to enter
the Guy Fawkes' competition on Bonfire Night.'

'But that's the competition to see who can make
the best Guy,' said Mrs Einstein. 'The child who
wins is allowed to light the big bonfire on the
village green.'

'I know,' smiled Dr Gooseberry.

'So isn't that a *bad* idea?' said Mr Einstein. 'We're
encouraging him to play with fire.'

'Not messecarily.' The Fire Lord
winked. 'It might be *good*. Suffice to say,
lady and gentleman, that you should do
exactly as I say and the cure will take care
of itself.' He paused for a sign that they
agreed to his terms, but none was
forthcoming. 'I can see you're dubilious, but don't
be,' he continued. 'Whatever Frank wants to do you
must let him do it.' Then he rubbed his hands and
kicked up his heels with excitement. 'Now, if you'll
excuse me, I've got a hot date waiting in the passion

...eer up! Victory will be ours!' And with
...ut asking for any sort of payment, the
...sappeared in a puff of smoke.

* * *

That night, when Frank was told what had been
decided, his face lit up.

'I'll make the best Guy this village has ever seen!'
he beamed.

'That's the idea,' said his father.

'And you promise, if I win you'll
let me light the big bonfire?'

His parents promised.

'Then I'm going to start tonight!' he gushed
excitedly.

And because his parents had been told to let him
do whatever he wanted, he was allowed to leave the
table without asking to get down, empty his
wardrobe into a black sack and rush off to their
allotment where Mr Einstein had a garden shed. For
the next few days this would be Frank Einstein's
laboratory where he would build himself a stuffed
man!

But life is never as simple as we'd like it to be.
Frank was not the only child in the village building
a Guy Fawkes dummy. Seventeen of the twenty

20

sheds on the allotments had **'TOP SECRET'** signs on the door, not to mention an array of Skull and Crossbones and warnings to **'KEEP OUT – GUY UNDER CONSTRUCTION'**. There was a run on essential Guy-building materials in the village causing a shortage of twine and straw, but Frank did not go without. Everything he asked for he was given, including his father's favourite hat and a brand new plastic football.

After a couple of days, however, it was clear that Frank was not happy. Gardeners heard screams of frustration from inside the shed and unrepeatable swear words. The trouble was that Frank's Guy didn't look like a man. It looked like what it was: two saggy compost sacks tied together with string. It had no arms or legs, which meant that the clothes didn't fit, and the football face looked like a crushed skull, because he'd foolishly used drawing pins for eyes. When Frank realised that he didn't have the skills to win the competition, it was a bitter pill to swallow. To add insult to injury, other children kept emerging from their sheds with beaming faces and skipping feet. Excited words tumbled from their mouths as they praised the beauty of their creations and chattered about

winning as if it was a foregone conclusion.

'It's spooky!' giggled a girl called Arabella. 'But my Guy's face is so life-like it's like there's a real person living in my shed!'

'Oh joy!' cried her parents. 'You truly are the apple of our eyes!'

Actually, *that* was Arabella's secret: other children had used parsnips for noses and sculpted potatoes for ears, but *only* Arabella had used apples for eyes.

The combined shock of *his* failure and the *other children's* success drove Frank to despair. His black moods and jealous rages stopped him from doing any further work on his Guy. It lay unfinished and abandoned on the floor. He spent his days huddled in the shed like a prisoner in solitary confinement, sitting by the window, watching his competitors come and go with new body parts; gloves for hands, wellingtons for feet and old string mops for hair. He sat and he brooded and schemed in his head.

* * *

By the evening of 4 November, twenty-four hours before the competition, Frank had a plan. As the bitter cold frosted the inside of the window pane, he sat in his shed waiting for nightfall. The only noise was the rhythmic swoosh of the whetstone as he sharpened the machete in his hand. If destroying the competition was the only way to win the right to light the bonfire, so be it. Between six and eight o'clock, the other children came to check their work. They made final adjustments, then locked their sheds and left the allotments. Frank watched them all depart. Now it was time.

Does anyone know what the time is?

Not that sort of time, Tom! Go back to sleep.

Thick clouds wrapped up the moon and plunged the allotments into darkness. As Frank switched on his torch and walked across the mud towards the first hut, a distant roll of thunder cleared its throat. He snapped the padlock with his crowbar and pulled the door towards him. Slumped in the corner of the shed was Arabella's Guy with its lifelike face and apple eyes. One flash of steel and the head was his. As he turned to leave, the decapitated figure slumped to the floor. Frank smiled, shut the door behind him and moved onto the next shed.

He broke into all sixteen sheds and stole what he needed to make his Guy look like a man. Then he massacred what remained of the competition to cover his tracks; fingers, heads, arms, lips, legs, ears and hair – all sliced up and gone. Back in his own shed, he set to with a needle and twine and sewed the stolen body parts onto his Guy, gifting it padded limbs, leather feet and hands, a pumpkin skull, apple eyes and a toothy smile cut from the skin of a blood red orange.

It was about this time that Mrs Einstein woke with a start and shouted out her son's name.

'FRANK!' Her face drained of colour as she sat bolt upright in bed.

'What is it?' mumbled Mr Einstein, forcing himself awake beside her.

'I saw his face!' she moaned.

'Whose face?' he said. 'Frank's?'

'No. The Fire Lord. He was in my dream.'

Did I mention that he's a good friend of mine?

'He took my hand and told me that everything was on course: that the electric storm had been ordered and it would not be long now till a permanent cure was found.'

'That's good, isn't it?' yawned Mr Einstein.

'It didn't sound good at all,' she shivered. 'There were flames licking out of his mouth.'

'Has there been a storm?' her husband mumbled comfortingly. 'No. You see . . .' Then he drifted back to sleep.

* * *

Frank tied off the final stitch and lowered the arm to the side of the body. His Guy was laid out on his father's workbench like a corpse on a mortuary slab. It looked a little freakish having been fashioned from several different sized bodies, but despite the large orange head it was impressively life-like.

Suddenly, a bolt of lightning ripped the black sky in two. Thunder crashed overhead and the shed shook as hailstones the size of quails' eggs tipped out of the sky and bounced off the roof. Frank rushed towards the window to see where this storm had come from, but before he had taken three steps a second flash of lightning hit the shed. Its jagged tip pierced the roof like a hypodermic needle, knocked Frank sideways and stabbed his Guy

Fawkes' dummy in its heart!

Frank picked himself up off the floor. He was lucky to be alive. He checked to see that his Guy was still intact by shaking its limbs and prodding its ribs. As he did so, the apples in the dummy's eyes seemed to flicker behind their eyelids. Were his own eyes playing tricks on him? He lowered his ear to the dummy's chest to listen for a breath, only to leap back like a scalded cat when the creature groaned. Then it opened its eyes, swung its stuffed legs off the worktable and stood up on its own two feet. As it swayed from side to side like a sleepy, six-foot scarecrow, Frank held his breath. He was expecting it to lunge for his throat and tear him limb from limb, but it did not move. It looked at Frank as a begging dog might look at its master.

The creature had the saddest face that Frank had ever seen. Its down-turned mouth and mismatched appled eyes (one red, one green) made it look as if it was permanently on the verge of tears.

'Can you speak?' he asked.

The creature nodded its heavy head. 'You must not judge me by the way I look,' it said.

'So you're *not* sad?' said Frank.

'Far from it,' replied the creature, pushing up the

corners of its mouth with one of its three fingers. 'How could I be unhappy when you have given me the legs to escape with?' And without another word it lurched towards the door.

'Where are you going?' shouted the boy.

'To escape the flames!' it cried. 'I don't want to burn tomorrow. I want to live and see the world.' By now it had twisted the handle, ducked under the door, and staggered across the mud outside.

'Get back in here!' screamed Frank. 'You're not going anywhere!'

Frank had just made a Guy Fawkes' dummy that could walk and talk. If that wasn't a sure-fire competition winner *nothing* was. He plunged into the hailstorm and grabbed the creature's arms.

'Give me my freedom!' it groaned, as Frank shoved it back inside the shed and locked the door to prevent any further escape attempts. 'Set me free!'

'No way,' smirked the boy. 'I made you to burn and burn you shall! I don't care if this hurts you to hear it, but I shall take great pleasure in setting fire to the bonfire myself!'

Upon hearing these words the creature started sobbing.

'Oh, come on!' chided Frank. 'It's only fire. You're a dummy stuffed with straw. It doesn't hurt.'

'Really?' said the creature, turning off the tears instantly, as if it had a tap in the side of its neck. 'It doesn't hurt?'

'No,' said Frank.

'So if you were me, you wouldn't *mind* being burned?'

'Of course I wouldn't,' said the boy carelessly. The creature sat up and without the aid of a forefinger stretched its orange peel mouth into the broadest grin that Frank had ever seen.

'Oh,' it said, placing a hand on the back of Frank's neck. 'Interesting!'

Now if this monster isn't a freak of nature I'm a monkey's uncle. And if I'm a monkey's uncle I'm the biggest freak of nature that ever lived!

* * *

The following morning, when Mr and Mrs Einstein went into Frank's bedroom, they were surprised to find him still in bed.

'Not working on your Guy today, Frank? You haven't forgotten that the competition's tonight, have you?'

'Yeah, I know,' mumbled the figure under the duvet.

'You sound a bit hoarse,' said Mrs Einstein. 'I'll take your temperature.'

'No!' came the sharp reply. 'I'm just tired. I'm going to stay in bed all day and get up for the competition tonight.'

Knowing how keen Frank was to light the bonfire, this lethargy struck Mr and Mrs Einstein as odd, but because they had to do everything their son wanted if he was to be permanently cured of fire-raising, they simply said, 'Fine,' and 'See you later.' And Mrs Einstein added as she left the room, 'When you get dressed be sure to wrap up warm. Last night was the coldest night since 1816.'

He stayed in bed all day so that nobody could see him. He faced the wall and listened to the bonfire being built on the village green; *his* bonfire; *his* match; *his* flames!

As dusk fell on the village, Frank got up, dressed in his warmest clothes and pulled a thick balaclava

over his head before leaving the house. When he arrived at the allotments there was a commotion. The other children had turned up to collect their Guys and discovered the midnight massacre. There were tears and tantrums as they cradled their butchered dummies in their hand, but it was nothing to do with Frank. He put his head down so that nobody could see his face, walked briskly through the screaming crowds and unlocked the shed.

* * *

It was like stepping into a refrigerator. Spending the night in freezing conditions had killed off any fight that the creature still had. It was lying on the floor where Frank had left it, every bit as perfect as the night before, except for the bump on its head of course and the frozen blood in its veins. He picked it up, pulled its hat down over its eyes and dragged it over to the judging table.

'My goodness!' exclaimed the man behind the table. 'Your Guy's intact. Well done, young man. Everyone else lost theirs last night. Terrible business. Name, please.'

'Frank Einstein,' he mumbled.

'Well, Frank, that is a splendid-looking Guy indeed. I don't think I've ever seen one so life-like. How on earth did you get the skin to look so real?'

The judge reached out to touch the dummy's cheek, but the boy pulled it away.

'Clingfilm and make-up,' he said.

'Really?' said the judge. 'It could almost be alive. First class job. Well, seeing as you're the only entrant, I can safely say that you are the winner. Put your Guy on top of the bonfire and here's your match.' It was as simple as that.

The bonfire was thirty feet tall. Frank climbed a ladder with the Guy on his back and sat it down on top of the wood.

'This is it then,' he said. 'This is where we say goodbye.' He tied the Guy's hands to a large log and climbed back down, drew the match across the striker with his three-fingered hand and let out a cry for freedom.

The bonfire crackled and squeaked with fire and smoke. Then with one look up from his appled eyes (one red, one green) he melted into the night amidst the 'Oohs!' and 'Aahs!' of the crowd. Not only was the creature free, but for one night only, Frank Einstein had the pleasure of sitting atop the biggest and brightest fire of his life.

And he found it very hot!

Help! I'm on fire!

What did I say? That's Frank shouting now. He lives down here in the Trophy Room. After the bonfire, I had him shovelled into a little wooden cup and once a year the Australian children and the English children play a cricket match and the winner gets to keep Frank's ashes for a year. Bit bizarre, but they seem to like it.

INTERESTING FACTS ABOUT LITERATURE
Number 6 – The Gooseberry Set

In his controversial autobiography *The Devil I Am!*, the Fire lord Lord Gooseberry (he's a really good friend of mine in case you didn't know) admitted that The Frank Einstein Cure was the most permanent that he'd ever dished out in his four thousand year career.

Lord Gooseberry's been my best friend ever since he came and did his party act for one of the kiddies' birthdays. It was very entertaining. As I recall, he started off with a few balloon animals — that's to say, he used a Bunsen Burner to inflate animals with hot air until they floated like balloons;

moved on to an unusual ventriloquist act in which he invited a demon to inhabit the children's bodies then made them swear like scaffolders in a really deep voice – that was funny; then finished up with his fire-eating act and burned down the curtains in the playroom!

He's my nearest neighbour, you know. Lives just below me. Many's the evening we've sat in a warm log fire and chewed the fat. I forget whose, but you can't beat a bit of crackling, can you?

If you think you've heard this next tale before that's probably because it's about recycling . . . about taking something worthless and turning it into something useful; turning it into something that might benefit mankind instead of sitting on mankind's backside like a monstrous carbuncle!

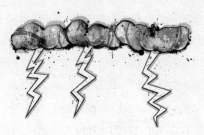

RECYCLOPS

Scabby was not a useful human being. She contributed nothing to the well-being of the planet. She wasn't a giver. She was a taker; a waster, a chucker-away. She consumed the earth's produce like a hyperactive vacuum cleaner and spat it out behind her when she no longer wanted it.

'You are so wasteful!' her mother screamed at her one Sunday, after Scabby had washed her hair and thrown away the full bottle of shampoo, then dried her hair with her mother's hairdryer and thrown *that* away too. 'I wish someone would waste you for a change!' Not a pleasant thing to say, but Scabby's mother was at the end of her tether.

Scabby's parents, Mr and Mrs Knees, were passionate recyclers. Nothing went to waste. They recycled everything from bottles and plastic to newspapers and grass cuttings. Anything that could be reused was put back into the system. They'd built their self-sufficient, eco-friendly house into the side of a hill with a lawn on the roof to trap the heat, an oven fired by chicken droppings, solar electricity, a human-powered rat-wheel-type lift (which saved on hardwood for the stairs), and a unique water recycling system that basically involved filtering pee and pumping it back through the taps.

'Glass of water, vicar?'

'Do you know, Mrs Knees, I think I'll just die of thirst, if you don't mind.'

Scabby's parents had even recycled their own names, Scott and Abi, to come up with Scabby. When they first heard this, Scabby's grandparents breathed a huge sigh of relief.

'Thank goodness they didn't recycle our names,' said Grandpa Walter.

'You can say that again,' replied Granny Millie.

So imagine their horror when their daughter turned out to be an exact opposite.

'Recycling is for dung beetles!' she'd say, as she chucked her bath towel in the dustbin. She was part of a disposable generation and could throw stuff away if she wanted. Easy come, easy go. The truth was she had the concentration span of a gnat.

Actually. that's not very flattering to gnats. because if you sit a gnat down in front of a three-minute film of an aphid doing rhythm gymnastics its attention doesn't waver at all.

* * *

Scabby always wanted something new and if that meant chucking out her old stuff to get it, that is what she did. When she was still in her pushchair she dropped things on the floor and 'forgot' to pick them up again: bibs, dummies, toys, sweets, shoes and chocolate Fairy Cakes fell out of her hands, never to be seen again. As she grew older, the objects she discarded became more expensive to replace. When she was five, for example, following a school trip to the swimming baths, she arrived back home in her bathing costume.

'Where are your clothes?' cried her mother.

'What are you talking about?' said Scabby, glancing down at her bare tummy. 'Oh dear. I must have lost them.' She hadn't lost them at all. She'd just left them in the cubicle, because she fancied a change. That was it: change. The driving force in Scabby's life. Change for change's sake.

As she grew older, she 'lost' stuff on a regular

37

basis: school books, packed lunches, dolls, cardigans, braces, bicycles and a tank full of stick insects.

'Not again!' cried her mother. 'That's the third tank of stick insects you've lost this week.'

'I didn't want them,' said Scabby. In fact, there were several reasons why she had thrown away the stick insects.

1. Holding the tank was proving inconvenient as she wanted to use her hands for something else (i.e. picking her nose).
2. It was sunny and she wanted to dance.
3. She wanted a gerbil instead . . . or a hamster, or a rabbit, or a spectacled bear.

This was how her mind worked. Always thinking about the next thing, instead of enjoying what she had.

She flung herself onto the reclaimed sofa, kicked off her socks and yawned. 'Anyway, who cares if I threw the stick insects away?' she continued. 'I can always get some more.'

It was this flippancy that got Mr Knees' goat. 'If you keep replacing stuff you don't *need* to replace, you're wasting the earth's resources,' he informed her. 'To help you learn this lesson, Scabby, I am putting you on washing-up duty for the next two weeks!'

Scabby laughed at the absurdity of his suggestion. She never helped around the house. It was too boring. Besides, her parents were a pair of softies. They set the rules but never enforced them. Scabby knew that she could waste the earth's resources as often as she liked, because nobody was ever going to stop her!

What she didn't know was that it wouldn't be a PERSON who would exact revenge on behalf of the planet, but a self-assembling, metal-hearted, hate-filled MACHINE!

* * *

One dark day, twenty-four hours after Scabby's tenth birthday, while the sun was swaddled in a nappy of clouds, Scabby woke up and decided to change her life *completely*!

'Lock, stock and barrel,' she announced, disappearing into her bedroom with a roll of black plastic sacks and a sledgehammer. 'Out with the old and in with the new!' Three hours later, she emerged with forty-six sacks of clothes and a huge pile of firewood. She took them out into the garden, loaded them onto a dog cart, and attached the dog cart to the back of her bicycle.

She was just setting off for the tip when her mother hurled herself across her path and stopped her. 'What are you throwing away now?' she cried.

'Everything,' said Scabby.

'But most of it's new!'

'So?' groaned the girl with the butterfly mind. 'I'm bored with it. I want to start again.'

Her mother picked up two pieces of splintered wood. 'This was your bed,' she said, 'and this was your wardrobe!'

'Past its hang-by date,' said Scabby glibly.

'Are you expecting us to replace it?' asked Mrs Knees.

'Of course,' said Scabby, standing up on her pedal and trying to push off. But her mother held onto the handlebars and cried out for help. Laying down his recycled newspaper with its recycled news, Mr Knees bounded from his moss-embroidered armchair and answered her call.

* * *

On a windswept dump not a million miles away, the

rubbish stirred: a twisted car panel, a metal motor from a tumble drier, a box of rusty knives and forks. As if drawn by an invisible magnet, they turned to face north and rolled up the fetid hill to its peak, where they met and joined together.

This is one of my famous poems, which if you are good at reading double meanings contains a clue as to the horrible fate what Scabby's got coming to her!

'Scabby'

Zup-Zup
Click-clack
It's a RUBBISH
Pay-back.

Unaware of the nasty surprise that lay just around the corner for her, Scabby slouched across the handlebars of her bike while her mother and father sifted through her bags of rubbish. Their gasps of disbelief came thick and fast.

'Have you gone *mad*, Scabby? You can't throw away *all* your clothes!'

'I've worn them once,' said Scabby, as if that made it all right. 'What more do you want?'

'This skirt took me months to crochet,' cried her mother.

'*Oh perlease!*' groaned Scabby. 'Time to move on. That skirt is so yesterday!'

'Only because we *gave* it to you yesterday!' snapped Mrs Knees, while Mr Knees pulled out a set of wooden coat hangers and stroked them.

'I whittled these from fallen branches,' he whispered.

'Well, I don't need them now I haven't got any clothes,' said Scabby. 'And I don't need *that* either.'

'Your wind-up radio!' gasped her mother. 'But it's brand new.'

'I don't care if it was made under a second ago by invisible imps! I'm bored with the tune it plays.'

'What do you mean *the* tune it plays? It plays hundreds of tunes,' said her father. 'You just have to find the right station.'

'Precisely,' she said grandly. 'Work, work, work! I'm not a slave . . .'

And with that, she snatched the objects out of her parents' hands, threw them back in the sacks, jumped onto the bike and set off for the end of the lane, where she piled the sacks high and left them for the dustbin men to collect in the morning.

Meanwhile, a broken-handled sledgehammer, a key-cutting lathe, the shattered headlamp of a vintage car, a buckled blade from a circular saw, a burnt-out industrial juicer and a wide-gauge drill bit for boring through bone, a whip, a wheel and a whale-tooth cudgel were all sucked across the dump by the invisible force and drawn together at a rush. Recalled from the grave, wrecked and rusting rubbish tumbled into its pre-determined position in the body of the metal junk giant that stretched towards the unseen sun.

* * *

When Scabby Knees arrived home she found her parents sitting on the sofa, crying. She had just trampled on everything that they held dear. In her lap, Mrs Knees was cradling a pair of white satin shoes.

'You forgot these,' she said quietly. 'My mother's wedding shoes that I wore for *my* wedding and have saved for *yours*.'

'Ugh!' said Scabby. 'Don't like those. Chuck them in the bin.'

This was the final straw. Rising from the sofa like a waking tiger, Mr Knees exploded. 'That's it! If you don't get back down that lane and retrieve all those rubbish sacks,' he seethed, 'I shall – I shall—'

'You shall *what*?' yawned Scabby. 'Recycle me?'

'Yes!' shouted her father. 'Yes! I shall call on Recyclops to come in here and recycle you!'

'I've heard it all before, Daddy! You're always threatening me with Recyclops, but has he ever come? No.'

'He'll burst in here with his cold metal heart, crush you with his pitiless piston-mitts and recycle you into something useful!'

'Recycled threat! I'm ten years old. It doesn't scare me any more.'

'I'll do it!'

'I don't think you will.'

'I'm doing it now!' yelled her father, his face turning red as he shouted out at the top of his lungs; 'Recyclops! Come hither!'

But Scabby just laughed. 'You are so pathetic,' she said. 'You think I don't know that you're telling me a little parent-lie to scare me into being a good girl. Well, it won't work.'

'Then go to your room!' shouted her mother.

'Gladly!' came the less-than-daughterly reply.

Unfortunately for Scabby, Recyclops only needed to be asked once. Her father's cry reached the rubbish tip as the sun was setting on a rotten world. The metal monster picked up the vintage-car headlamp with the tips of its spaded fingers and crushed it into the hole in the middle of its forehead. Gouts of black engine oil squirted down its face as it twisted and locked the headlamp into position. At last, Recyclops could see!

* * *

The one-eyed robot with the strength of fifteen garbage trucks scraped itself up off the heap. Its armoured body creaked and screeched like a car in a crusher as it pulled itself up to its full height. Then it lowered its four-wheeled undercarriage, reclaimed from an old Silver Cross pram, and recycled off to Scabby's house.

It was night-time when it arrived to exact its retribution, clanking down the lane like a cybernetic Samurai. Scabby was asleep on her floorboards when Recyclops absorbed the brickwork into its own body and stepped through the wall of her bedroom. Then it bundled her up with a ball of blue twine and took her off to its recycling plant.

Scabby was dropped into a vat of soapy water, run through a mangle and stretched out like a sheet of pink paper. She was steamed, pressed, powdered and pinched, lightly simmered in a vat of glue (to hold her limbs on) and thunderised with lightning. All of this before she had her heart restrung, her stomach repiped, her voice retuned and her body reshaped. Recyclops popped her into a furnace for a final meltdown, then poured her out of a copper jug into a biodegradable mould and reconstituted her body into its original shape.

When she woke up, Scabby did not know where she was. She was lying on a cold table under the glare of four bright lights. If she turned her head to one side she could see that she was in some sort of factory. Heavy machinery lined the white walls and hissed like containers full of snakes. Suddenly the door burst open at the far end of the room. In a blast of steam and the turn of a wheel Recyclops was by her side. Before she could even scream she was tangled up in a cargo net fired from the monster's wrist, while something cold and fishy switched her lights out. It was a cast iron punch from Recyclops' fist and the knuckles were made from sardine tins. Her body ached.

Only this time it had one or two special features!

46

'You monster!' she cried. 'What have you done to me?'

'Monster yourself!' replied Recyclops in a voice it had recycled from a Dalek. 'I've done you a favour. I have turned you into a useful member of the human race!'

And it was true, Scabby now had a tap in her armpit so that she could water the garden, a motor in her mouth to make her suck dirt like a vacuum cleaner, a siren in her throat to turn her into a early-warning fire alarm, magnetic legs for picking up litter, a paint-filled scalp for decorating the house, telescopic fingernails containing an assortment of handy tools, Wheelie Knees (an ingenious arrangement of wheels and hinges that turned her into a shopping trolley), extendable feet converting speedily into water-skis to save old sailors in distress, a bouncy belly to turn her into a bean bag and, at night, she folded up into a box for handy storage in the attic.

This was the feature her parents liked best. It meant that every night they simply packed her away and popped her in the loft. And this meant that she didn't need her bedroom anymore, so they rented it out to students and made a bit of extra money on the side, which was a perfect way to recycle the wasted space in the house!

Scabby works in this hothell now as a scullery maid.

I don't want to be useful!

That's all she ever says these days; over and over and BLINKING over like a broken record. I wish she WAS a record. I could melt her in the oven and recycle her as a vinyl snack tray.

In the Darkness children are a huge source of recyclable material and I make use of them whenever I can, as my well-deserved green ticket proves.

THE GREEN TICKET
Awarded to people who have made a major contribution to the clearing up of our environment.
**FOR HIS SELFLESS CLEARANCE OF HUMAN RUBBISH OUT OF HOMES AND SCHOOLS
THE NIGHT-NIGHT PORTER**
has been made a

GOLD MEMBER!

This card has been printed on recycled eyelids

The heating in this hothell is run entirely on recycled guests. The bigger children compress really efficiently into briquettes which stoke the child-burning stoves. while the little babies are great for heating up the hot water. I make them drink gallons of orange squash, remove their nappies, dump them in the hot water tank and let them peel

---

INTERESTING FACTS ABOUT NATURE
Number 607 – The Weather
We don't get weather down here in the Hothell Darkness.

Actually, that's not true. In Room 987, a lazy shepherd boy who fell asleep and let his sheep be eaten by wolves has got a dog called Weather. So I should have said that in the Darkness good weather is weather that fetches a stick and drops it at your feet when you ask it to, whereas bad weather just lies on its back and wants its tummy tickled. It wouldn't have made a lot of sense though, would it?

Still, the place they really like their weather is in the countryside. They're full of old weather sayings up there.

This forecast about the weather
Is Old and Cold don't go together
(Like fox and chick with downy feather)
So if perchance you get the itch
To leave your Gran without a stitch
(Having filched her shawl with a fishing flitch)
Watch out for storms from the Weather Witch.

Of course, some children think this old country saying is a load of mumbo jumbo and refuse to heed its message, which is treat old people and the weather with respect or answer to the Weather Witch. Well here's a Newsflash.

NEWSFLASH NEWSFLASH NEWSFLASH NEWSFLASH

'CHILDREN WHO THINK THIS OLD COUNTRY
SAYING IS A LOAD OF MUMBO JUMBO AND
REFUSE TO HEED ITS MESSAGE ARE DEAD MEAT.'

OR, AS ANOTHER OLD COUNTRY SAYING
PUTS IT . . .

COCKY KIDS WHO TEASE THE OLD
SHALL REAP A WHIRLWIND, STRENGTH UNTOLD.

THE WEATHER WITCH

It is a well-known fact that bitterly cold weather can actually freeze the human heart until it stops beating. Interestingly, people with frozen hearts don't actually die, they just become mean instead – a meanness born of the excruciating pain caused by the petrification of the muscles in the heart when they spontaneously turn into stone. It stands to reason, therefore, that people who spend all their time in freezing cold temperatures are more likely to be mean; ice hockey players, for example, or traffic wardens, or bored little boys who roam the winter streets with nothing better to do than pick on old people for fun!

I know who you are!

It was the middle of a long, cold winter when a boy

51

called Jack Frost began his cold-hearted reign of terror. It started with snowballs aimed at old-age-pensioners' hats as they slid home from the Post Office, and quickly progressed to snow-cannonballs, fired from a three-metre wooden catapult that Jack had built in the garden. If properly aimed he could take out up to ten old people with one shot, which was why he called his sick little game Ten Pin Bolding.

At night he crept into their front gardens and watered their paths with a watering can. By morning the water had frozen causing the elderly residents to slip on the ice and slide down the paths on their bottoms. Jack liked to score their slides with score cards.

'Nine for artistic impression,' he cheered over the old lady's screams of terror. 'Next time, don't look so scared and I'll give you a ten!'

He organized wheelchair ballets on strips of black ice in the supermarket car park. It was simple. He would hang around the aisles until he saw an old person in a wheelchair distracted by a special offer on tea, for example, or marble cake, then he'd rush up behind them, grab their chairs and push them into the car park, where he had Tchaikovsky's

Nutcracker Suite playing on an iPod. Then he'd spin the wheelchair on the ice in time with the music and rush back inside to get another wheelchair before the first one stopped spinning.

Unsurprisingly, the stream of complaints to Jack's parents was constant. So much so that after the *Nutcracker*-on-Ice incident Jack's mother grounded him.

'Until spring!' she cried.

'Spring!' exclaimed Jack. 'But that's three months away.'

'You're not going out until the snow has melted,' said his father.

'And the first daffodil has poked its tiny yellow head above the soil,' added Mrs Frost.

'If it pokes its head anywhere near me I shall stamp on it,' said Jack. 'You don't really think you can keep me in, do you?'

'Of course,' said his father. 'We'll be watching you like hawks!'

His parents *tried* to watch Jack like hawks, but they weren't trained prison guards and they didn't have CCTV cameras pointing at every window in the house. One Tuesday evening, while Mr Frost was having his late-afternoon snooze and Mrs Frost was letting her hair down at bingo, Jack built a decoy snowman. He sat the snowman at his desk with his homework book in front of it, dressed it in his clothes, and jumped out of the window. Later, when his parents came in to say goodnight, they gasped with shock. They had both noticed a puddle of water under Jack's chair.

'Oh dear,' cried his mother. 'Have you had an accident, Jack?' There was no response so she shook her son by the shoulders. 'Jack?'

But his head rolled off.

'Aaaaaaaagh!'

Jack heard her scream half a mile away. He was up on the roof of the old folk's home pretending to be Santa. Instead of pushing presents down the chimney, however, he was shovelling in snow to put out their fire.

'Ho ho ho!' he boomed down the flue. Then, when he heard the cries of anguish from below, 'Ha ha ha!'

* * *

The next day, when Jack's parents discovered that he hadn't actually lost his head or melted into his bedroom floor, they forgave him. They were so pleased their son hadn't turned into a puddle that they lifted their grounding order and let him out again.

'Told you!' he crowed cockily as he rushed out the front door. 'These walls cannot hold me!'

Jack rushed off to the steep hill in the park with his toboggan. At the bottom of the hill was a frozen duck pond. A wooden sign on the bank warned, **'THIN ICE! NO SKATING!'**

Most tobogganists stopped well short of the ice, but Jack had waxed his runners for maximum speed, which meant that his first run was nearly his last. He came down the slope like a bullet, shouting abuse at the young children in his path and scattering them into the snow drifts on either side of the run.

'Gangwaaaaaaaay!' He was having so much fun terrorising the toddlers that he didn't notice when he overshot the wooden sign. By the time he looked up it was too late. He was heading towards the thin ice and a cold, watery grave.

Suddenly, a small tornado of snow corkscrewed up in front of him, and an old woman with glittering hair and fingernails dressed entirely in white, popped up from nowhere. She held out her hand like a traffic cop. A cold gust of wind blew from her fingertips and stopped Jack in his tracks.

'Take care!' she whispered in a voice that echoed from the clouds. 'You are skating on thin ice.'

'Are you blind?' he sneered. 'I'm nowhere near the ice. I'm standing on snow.'

'If you go on the ice, Jack, you will die.' Jack pushed her away. She was old and she was bothering him. 'I am fed up with people barging into my life and telling me what to do. How do *you* know what's best for me?'

'Because I can see the future,' she said. 'And if you don't change, Jack, it's a future that looks rather short.'

'What are you?' snorted Jack. 'Some sort of witch?'

'A Weather Witch,' she said. 'You'll find us everywhere – in the clouds and the sunshine, the fog and the rain.'

'I hope you're not expecting me to be scared,' he jeered, 'because I'm *not*!'

'Go home!' she said firmly. 'Before it's too late.' She laid a hand on his shoulder to turn him around, but Jack batted it off.

'I don't need your crumbly

advice,' he shouted. 'You're an interfering old busybody. I can look after myself!'

'Then remember this,' smiled the wrinkled lady in white. 'Respect is free.' Her words were swept up in a flurry of snow as she span back into the ether. 'I'm watching you.'

But Jack was not going to change his ways for a batty old stranger. Even if she could see into the future, it wasn't *his* future. There was only *one* person in charge of Jack's life and that was Jack.

* * *

So Jack *didn't* change. He spent another night on the prowl. First, he crept down to Bill the Bag's shed on the allotments and tied fishing lines around the icicles which were hanging down from the roof above his door. Then he knocked and waited for old Bill to climb out of his camp bed and answer. As the door opened, Jack tugged on the fishing lines. The icicles snapped off and fell like glass daggers through the toes of Bill's slippers, pinning his feet to the ground.

'Got you!' screamed Jack. 'Now you'll have to wait for the thaw before you can go back to bed!'

Leaving Bill standing out in the cold, Jack moved

on to Miss Tremble's cottage where he packed snow around her water pipes. The following morning, Miss Tremble was discovered iced into her bath. She had been in there for seven hours and was only rescued when a bout of extreme chattering caused her false teeth to shoot out of her mouth, fly through the window and land on the pavement below. Thankfully, a passer-by picked them up, tried them on, realized they weren't theirs and called the police. But old Miss Tremble nearly died.

> Don't string me up!

> I wonder if that would work for Jack? By the way, that's William shouting. He's a bit conkers.

The next night, the Weather Witch returned. Jack was tired after missing a whole night's sleep and had decided to stay indoors. He was sitting on the sofa watching a weather report when the weatherman's face seemed to melt and re-form into the craggy features of the witch.

'So expect high winds—' he was saying, as his voice slid up two octaves, '—and thunder and lightning. And if your name is Jack, expect a stormy night!'

'Did you hear that?' cried Jack. 'Was that just me or did he . . . or she . . . or whatever that weather person-thing is on the telly, just speak to me?'

'Didn't hear a thing,' said his mother.

Outside, the wind gusted, the snow flurried and thick yellow clouds, as livid as old bruises, rolled in from the North.

Two hours later, Jack was asleep when his window latch clicked open. A grey, stinking fog seeped into the room and floated towards the bed like a wraith. When it reached the sleeping boy, it gathered itself into the shape of the witch, who leaned forward and grasped Jack's heart with her icy fingers. He woke with a start, gasping for breath.

'You!' he yelled.

The Weather Witch was floating above his face like a cloud. 'You think it is funny to be old and cold,' she whispered, tightening her grip on his ticker.

'I can't breathe.' She lifted him off his mattress until their noses were touching.

'You really don't think that the cold can kill a person?'

'I don't kill them!' he cried. 'Old people love my

games. It's the only entertainment they ever get. It's a laugh!'

She uncurled her hand from his heart and Jack fell back onto his bed. 'Then you'll enjoy what I've got in store for you!' she cackled as her vaporised breath froze in mid-air. 'I'm going to show you what it's like to be cold! Colder than you've ever been before!'

With a flick of her fingers the temperature dropped by thirty degrees. Outside, a polar wind roared as the window snapped open and Jack was sucked out of bed into a freezing whirlwind. The Weather Witch had created an Ice Age in Jack's backyard. A leaping cat caught in the blizzard was locked into the landscape like an ice sculpture, frozen trees shed their leaves like metal death stars.

'Cold?' howled the Weather Witch.

'No,' shivered Jack, who was not going to be beaten by an old woman.

'Can you feel the pain in your bone marrow yet?'

'I'm tougher than you think,' he mumbled through stiff, blue lips. 'I'm not scared of anything!'

'Not even this?' Jack felt the earth rumble beneath his feet. Suddenly it opened up and a massive iceberg shot out of the ground and rushed towards the sky with Jack perched on top clinging for his life. His scream bounced back off the clouds.

'Not even that!' he bellowed from the top of the ice mountain. Then with a large dose of bravado, he added. 'That was fun!'

That'll be a NEW definition of 'fun', then!

fun / n. very scary.

Not for long. There was a roar over Jack's shoulder. He turned quickly to see the slavering muzzle of a sabre-toothed tiger. Its nostrils flared with the rich, heady scent of its prey. Jack's heart thumped as he searched for something to defend himself with. He grabbed two thick icicles and holding them like daggers ran towards the beast, deftly swerving like a matador to avoid its outstretched paw and thrusting the ice daggers into its neck. They crumbled on impact, as the tiger flicked its tail and roared. Jack was cat meat unless he jumped over the edge!

Closing his eyes he ran towards the sky. Then with a cry of 'Can't catch me, kitty!' he leapt into the unknown. His guess paid off. The ice face was *not* sheer. There was a hidden slope just over the first ridge for him to slide down. He had barely reached half-way, however, when he heard a giant roar from behind, looked up and saw the sabre-toothed tiger leap after him. Jack fell to earth with a bone-crunching thud and rolled to one side just in time, as the plummeting big cat hit the ground at sixty miles an hour and broke both its front teeth.

> There's another old country saying:
>   When a sabre tooth tiger loses its gnashers
>   Its food is prepared by electrical mashers.

'Is that the best you can do?' Jack said cockily, as the Weather Witch materialised in front of him like a windblown, muslin sheet.

'No,' she smiled. Then she span like a tornado and disappeared into the ice. Steam billowed from the hole that she had just drilled and Jack was drawn forward to peer over the edge. As he did so, the witch burst out of the hole and grabbed him by his neck.

'Now what do you see?' she asked, thrusting his head over the void. Something large was trapped inside the ice. Before Jack could make out what it was, the ice coffin ruptured at the seams and a mammoth was forced out of its glacial grave. Jack was tossed into the air and landed across the beast's neck. He tried to cling on to its matted fur, but the creature lowered its head and shook Jack off. He slipped down its trunk and was tossed to the ground by a tusk. Then the mammoth roared and bore down on the tiny boy like a wild, woolly truck with no brakes.

Jack turned and ran. He had a plan. If he could lure the beast onto the pond he might stand a chance.

'Come on, you dead mop of a dinosaur!' he yelled, trying to sound braver than he felt. 'Let's see if you're hard enough!'

But the cold must have numbed Jack's brain, because as he slid across the thin ice and the mammoth jumped on behind him, he suddenly realized that he hadn't thought his plan through.

The ice fractured with a sound like a ricocheting rifle shot. Cracks spread across the white surface like veins of black blood, before the ice suddenly gave way and the boy was plunged into water so cold that it took his breath away. The mammoth was also fighting for its life. It thrashed the water with its tusks and broke up the ice into tiny pieces, far too tiny to support the weight of a boy. With nothing to hold on to, Jack had to tread water. Not for long. In a matter of seconds his heart froze and a cold watery hand closed around him. The last thing he heard, as he floated to the bottom of the lake, was the Weather Witch's voice bubbling down from the sky like a chilled mountain stream.

'Cold enough now?' it said.

Four hours later, the sun was shining when Jack was pulled out of the pond. It was strange the way the Ice Age had blown over as quickly as it had arrived, only to be replaced by a tropical heat wave. It was as if the weather was somehow *not real*. But it was, because when Jack was winched out of the water he was frozen solid in a big block of ice, his face captured in a priceless moment of surprise.

* * *

Jack's parents had two choices. They could opt for a stress-free life by keeping their son in the freezer or they could thaw him out and hope that he'd learned a lesson. It was a close call, but in the end blood was thicker than water and they thawed him out in the greenhouse where the glass doubled the heat of the sun's rays.

But when he emerged from the giant ice cube, Jack was no longer made of flesh and blood. The cold that had frozen his heart had frozen the blood in his veins too and turned him into ice.

'Oh, silly Jack!' whispered his mother as she gently kissed his cheek. His face was cold. His minutes were numbered.

The Weather Witch was nearly done. Just one more job to do.

The sun burned hotter and hotter as she pushed the fiery orb higher into the sky. And as the temperature climbed, Jack Frost slowly dripped away.

When Jack first came down to this hothell I didn't know where to keep him. I put him in the swimming pool, thinking he'd want to be with other kids who were like him. He's not the first child who's ended up melting. Unfortunately I lost him and it took me five weeks of filtering to find him again. Then I kept him in a kettle, but he complained about the heat, so now I keep him in a bird bath where

Weather the Sheepdog drinks him, swills him around in his bladder and pees him into the flower bed! Jack's worried that there'll come a day, after I've been watering the garden, for example, when I won't be able to find him again. I've told him not to worry. 'I'll always recognise you,' I told him. 'You'll be the only puddle shouting, 'I'm not ccccold!' That shut the whinger up!

> I don't want to be useful!

I wish I could shut Scabby up. Maybe I should give her what she wants and turn her back into something USELESS. Trouble is I can't make my mind up what it should be; a chocolate teapot, a crocodile's dentist or a geography teacher?

> Don't string me up!

Now she's got everyone going. That's conker—bonkers William again in the Threading Room. Tragic really, the effect conkers can have on some children. They get addicted. Those little brown nuts wreck their lives. Some boys have got factories at home where they soak their conkers in vinegar to make them harder than rock. But William's the only boy I know who goes out at night to harvest whole wood-loads. He reasons thus; if he collects all of the conkers in the village nobody else can have any. and if nobody else has got any conkers there can be only one Conker King. namely the only person with a conker   him. It's not exactly bow-down-to-the-genius. but it does work.

Unfortunately for him I also know a strange man (no relation) who goes out at night and harvests whole bed-loads of naughty children. He reasons thus: if he collects all of the naughty children in the world and locks them up in a SCARY place to teach them a lesson they will NEVER EVER EVER forget. the world becomes a nicer place to live in .
. . Plus. he gets to soak the children in vinegar

 before threading their skulls with knotted string and bashing their heads together!

Now that's what I call clever!

I wonder who this strange man is though! Hmmmmmmmm – can't think.

I don't want to be useful!

Don't string me up!

68

WILLIAM THE CONKERER

William wasn't much liked by other kids. Not just because he nicked all the conkers in the village, but because they thought he was weird. He spent hours alone in the woods breaking the trees: tearing off branches, stripping their bark and carving his name in their trunks. William cared nothing for Nature. He had a list on his bedroom wall which showed, in descending order, the most important things in his life, and Nature was down at number twelve after *William* (1), *Conkers* (2), *Candy Lips* (8) and *Smelly trainers* (11). The point was that William considered himself *more* important than trees.

Squirrels are the same.

He could take what he liked from them without so much as a please or a thank you.

One autumn, however, on the very first day of the conker season, he took more than his fair share and Mother Nature made him pay!

In the best traditions of a William Conker Hunt, he set his alarm for midnight and was out in the woods by one. By the searching light of a high-beamed torch he picked missiles off the forest floor and chucked them at the Horse-chestnut trees until he had cleared their branches of conkers. Then, as dawn fast approached and laden with shiny brown booty, he pushed his wheelbarrow home through a battlefield of smashed-up twigs and branches.

On the village green, just in front of the cricket pavilion, was an ancient Horse-chestnut that reputedly had been planted in the reign of King Charles I. It was much revered, despite the fact that it had not produced a single conker since 1815 when Wellington defeated Napoleon at the Battle of Waterloo. So imagine William's surprise when he pushed his wheelbarrow past this tree, happened to glance up and there hanging off the highest branch was a big, green, spiky conker. There was no way William was going home without it!

It was, however, extremely high up. To knock it down would take a throw of unimaginable power and accuracy. For such a throw he would need the perfect missile.

There were no broken sticks or rocks on the well-tended green, so he looked for something else. He threw and missed with a **DO NOT WALK ON THE GRASS** sign, then tried his luck with a dead hedgehog and a doggy dustbin. All three hit the tree, smashed the branches and chipped away at the bark, but they also crashed back to earth and in the case of the doggy dustbin showered William with its contents.

Who's a lucky boy!

The large conker, however, stayed exactly where it was.

So William broke into the cricket pavilion and helped himself to a bat and several balls. Then he stood under the conker and belted cricket balls up at it, but this second wave of missiles also fell short. To make matters worse they smashed the lower branches and deluged him with broken twigs and tree bugs. William decided that he needed a catapult to fire his missiles into the tree.

He dragged the seesaw over from the

playground, then went back for the seats of the swings which were made out of car tyres. He'd seen tumblers do something similar in the circus. He piled the tyres on one end of the seesaw, shinned up the trunk, edged out along a thick branch and jumped. His idea was to land on the other end of the seesaw and flick the tyres high into the tree to reach the conker. Unfortunately, the tyres were heavier than William. On landing, the seesaw snapped with a loud bang, firing a splinter of wood deep into the bark of the tree like a piece of steel shrapnel.

* * *

William was desperate. Luckily, he lived with his grandfather, who happened to work at the car breaker's yard on the edge of the village. It was William's last chance. He ran to the yard, climbed over the gate, searched under the mat for the keys, opened the office, rifled the drawers and eventually found a four-digit code for the padlock on the cage where the heavy machinery was stored.

Ten minutes later with a large fridge/freezer swinging off a chain like a wrecking ball, William burst through the gates of the yard at the wheel of a mobile crane. Its caterpillar tracks tore up the grass on the village green as he manoeuvred it into position alongside the tree. Then he extended the crane's arm as far as it would go and by turning it first left then right and building up the momentum, he soon had the fridge/freezer swinging in mid air. The chances of scoring a direct hit on the conker were slight, so William took the easier option and repeatedly slammed the fridge/freezer into the trunk until the top of the tree sheared off. As it crashed to the ground, the conker was knocked from its branch and bounced to the ground at William's feet.

It was huge. When William lifted up the green spiky shell it was bigger than the palm of his hand. It had 'Conker King' written all over it! So keen was he to get it open that he tore at the shell with his teeth. Imagine his disappointment, therefore, when he finally split the casing apart only to find the teeniest tiniest conker inside. It was no bigger than a pea.

'That's rubbish,' he said, and he chucked it away without a second thought for all the damage he'd just done. Then he returned the crane to the yard and took his conkers back to bed.

> Does anyone know what the time is?

> Yes. It's time you put a sock in it. Tom!

* * *

Next morning, the village was in uproar. Not only had the wood been stripped of all its conkers, but when people opened their curtains and saw their beloved Horse-chestnut, they were horrified. It lay smashed and in ruins, its dying leaves drifting to the ground like feathered tears.

One leaf, however, was blown into the woods, where it settled on a branch outside a tree-house. Inside there lived a hermit gardener, a withered marrow of a man reputed to have not the *greenest* fingers in the world, but the *reddest* . . . for reasons that will soon become most shockingly clear!

> I'll give you a clue:
>
> Violence is red
> Dead lips are blue
> Behold it's a conker
> With a kiss made of glue!

* * *

At school that day, William was crowned Conker King, but only because nobody else had a conker to fight him with. It was a hollow victory that no one applauded. The rumour was that *he* had caused the damage to the ancient Horse-chestnut, but nobody could prove it. The accusation remained unspoken until Ashton Crow could hold his tongue no longer.

'You're just a greedy spoilsport,' he said to William in the lunch queue.

'And why would that be?' sneered William.

'For wrecking the village tree and spoiling the conker harvest for the rest of us.'

'I hope you can support your wild accusations,' William smirked, 'because I really don't know what you're talking about!' Then he patted the bulge of conkers in his blazer pocket and ordered a pine nut pizza.

That night, however, while William slept, Nature reared her not-so-pretty little head!

* * *

William was woken by the thump of a wooden ladder as it hit the wall outside his window. The rungs creaked as a pair of feet climbed up towards

75

him, then a knuckle tapped on the glass.

'Open up, young man.' The soft West Country burr encouraged William to trust it. He pulled back the curtain to see a smiling face beyond the window. It had red cheeks and a scraggy white beard that tapered to a point at his chest.

'Who are you? What do you want?' asked William.

'I'm a gar-dinner,' said the stranger.

Clocking the man's threadbare jumper and muddy wellington boots, William opened the sash window. 'Oh, a gardener!' he said.

'No. Not a gardener. A gar-*dinner*. Dinner, see? The dinner part's the most important, because that is why I is known to have red fingers not green.' The man scratched the side of his nose with a long red finger and chuckled.

'I don't care what colour your fingers are,' said William, 'what are you doing at my window in the middle of the night?'

'I have brought you a present,' he said, 'from the forest.' Seemingly from nowhere the gar-dinner produced a plastic plant pot. Poking up in the middle of the soil was a single green shoot. 'I can grow anything,

right, so long as it's a Giant Canadian Conker, which is what I happen to have in this here pot.' The stranger on the ladder pushed it across the window ledge.
'It's all yours,' he said.

'Did you say the *Giant* Canadian Conker?' queried William.

'That I did. Is there a problem?'

'Well, it's not very big, is it?'

'Not yet,' chuckled the gar-dinner. 'But it will be. It'll be the biggest conker in the world, on account of what it eats.'

'Eats?' For some reason the gar-dinner got a fit of giggles. His shoulders shook so much that William thought he was going to fall off the ladder.

'This here is a man-eating conker,' he wheezed.

William's eyes lit up with excitement. 'A *man*-eating conker?'

'Oh yes *indeed*,' continued the gar-dinner. 'It can eat a man whole. Bish-bosh, all gone! It's quite safe, though, as long as you never touch it directly with your skin.'

'You mean I should wear gloves?'

'That's it, because if you touches it directly with your fingers it won't let you go. It'll suck you in. Hand first, then your arm, then your entire body slurped up into its sticky heart where you'll be digested like a worm.'

The thought of a giant conker eating someone alive appealed to William. 'Could I use it to eat Ashton Crow?' he asked.

The gar-dinner nodded his head and smiled. 'Oh yes, there's all manner of uses for the Giant Canadian Conker,' he said.

<u>Uses For A Giant Canadian Conker</u>

Space Hopper

Heavy weight for drowning undesirables

Seafaring Globe (must be painted to look like a Seafaring Globe or it will never be more than a conker)

Melon frightener (without exception, all melons feel inferior next to a Giant Canadian Conker)

Contents of Sock-cosh for bank robber

Dog exerciser – stand dog on top of conker, issue order to 'Stay!' then push firmly down hill.

'Now, you'll need a few maintenance tips. This plant's a bit different from others, right. It grows at night by the light of the moon, so leave it on this ledge and always keep the window open.'

'Grows at night?'

'At night, yes. Like a vampire.'

'With the window open?'

'That's the important bit.' Then the gar-dinner tugged his forelock, wished William, 'Happy gar-dining!' and was gone, sliding down the ladder with the speed of a crippled lift plummeting down a shaft.

The Giant Canadian Conker grew fast and William was careful never to touch it with his bare hands. He wore his grandmother's rabbit skin gloves whenever he watered the plant, and left them on the window ledge every night. On the morning  of the third day they had mysteriously disappeared. William searched high and low, but they were nowhere to be found. The plant had grown though. In fact, it was growing so fast that William could lie on his bed and watch the leaves expand before his eyes.

By the end of the first week the giant conker was

fully grown and smacking its lips. It did not have a green, spiky shell as you might expect. The brown conker simply grew off the stem of the plant like a head . . . and grew and grew and grew. William noticed the tongue on the morning of the seventh day. It shot out through a hole in the shiny skin when he accidentally brushed the conker with his forearm.

'You're ready!' he grinned. 'Tomorrow you and I will go into school and ask Ashton Crow if he wants to stroke you!' The thought of Ashton Crow's face when the conker grabbed his hand and consumed his flesh convulsed William with laughter.

But William was suffering under the misapprehension that he was in charge of his own fate. Ashton Crow was *not* the intended victim. Ashton Crow did not vandalise trees. The gardinner had no beef with him.

That night, while William slept and the giant conker soaked up moonrays through the open window, the red-fingered gar-dinner returned to finish the job. This time, he was wearing thick gardening gloves and instead of wellington boots, a pair of soft, pink ballet pumps to muffle his footsteps. As he clambered through the open window, he scooped up the plant pot and tied a long piece of string around the conker's neck. Then, standing on a chair, he wound the other end of the string around the light bulb in the middle of the room. When he had finished the Giant Canadian Conker was hanging directly over William's chest, about two feet higher than his head.

'William,' he whispered. 'Oh William! How's about you and I have a game of giant conkers? I'll use this one hanging here, and you—' he muffled a laugh '—well *you* can use your head.'

Then the red-fingered gar-dinner clapped his hands. William's eyes pinged open at the noise and when he saw who was standing at the end of his bed he sat up with surprise. So quickly did he spring to the vertical that his forehead nutted the conker with a resounding thud. 'Strike one!' cheered the gar-dinner. 'First hit to you!' But when William went to pull his head away, the giant conker was stuck to his skin. A silent dinner bell

rang in the forest as the gar-dinner circled William's bed and stroked the giant conker. 'And now it's my turn,' he said. 'I think it likes you!'

'What's going on?' cried William. He

tried to pull the Giant Canadian Conker off his forehead, but his fingers stuck to its shell and started to melt. Nature had him by the throat. As his face turned to glue, the red-fingered gar-dinner laughed like a machine gun, danced across to the window and hopped back out onto his ladder.

'Good night, tree-killer,' he said, then disappeared from view as the conker's digestive sap trickled into William's heart and spread through his body like poison.

* * *

In the morning, William's grandmother found a giant conker lying on her grandson's pillow where his fat head should have been. And when she picked it up with her bare hands it said in a voice that sounded exactly like the voice of the red-fingered gar-dinner: 'Hello breakfast.'

It might seem cruel, but the Giant Canadian Conker does not distinguish between good people and bad people. People are food and a giant conker's got to eat. Ten seconds after picking up the conker, William's grandmother discovered what the voice had meant, when the nut brown killer attached itself to her face like a leech.

You won't be surprised to hear that William never conkered another tree again. This was due entirely to the fact that for the first time in his life a tree had conkered him!

The Giant Canadian Conker that ate William has retired now with a deadly score of sixty-three children and one granny to its name. It works down here in the Darkness as part of my entertainment team, helping me organise games of ten-pin bowling. We've invented this slightly different version of the game in which the conker lies absolutely still amongst the bowling balls until one of the children touches it. Then it jumps up, shouts 'Boo!' and eats them. Great fun!

A WORD OF WARNING!

If you're one of Nature's vandals and are rubbing your hands, because the man-eating conker's retired from active duty stop rubbing. It's not the ONLY Giant Canadian Conker in the world. Not by a long tongue. The red-fingered gar-dinner's got

THOUSANDS of the little suckers, and every night before he turns in he sings to them to make them grow.

> 'I am a jolly gar-dinner
> With fingers coloured red,
> From all the blood
> Wot's on my hands
> From keeping conkers fed!'

Nice!

> Does anyone know what the time is?

On and on like a broken record. It's nearly time for terror, Tom. Nearly time for you to wet yourself with fear!

 Of course, the Giant Canadian Conker isn't the only plant to grow to a freakish size. Look at the beanstalk that Jack grew, or the peach that James went around the world in. It's not natural, is it? Personally, I blame the scientists who spend their lives trying to control Mother Nature. As if you could just slap an ASBO on her! Ridiculous!

HEAR NO WEEVIL, SEE NO WEEVIL

It used to be the case that from little acorns did mighty oaks grow, but not any more. Nowadays, thanks to genetic modification, mighty hat stands can be grown from acorns. They're very clever chaps, these modern scientists. Now that they can manipulate genes it's only a matter of time before they create a hairy man ape from a handful of house dust. The trouble is that once they've done that it won't be enough. The scientists will have to create a hairless woman ape from a bar of soap, a lumpy boy ape from smelly trainers and a giggling girl ape from the problem page of *American Girl*. And where will this genetically modified family live? In a house made from a shoebox, with carpets grown on the backs of gorillas, eating three-course meals fashioned from that thick crust of gunk around the top of a ketchup bottle, drinking water matured from a single molecule of bison sweat, sleeping in hand-reared beds that need feeding at four hourly intervals, reading books created from the first word of a Roald Dahl novel, watching TV on a flat screen that started life as a supermodel and driving a car bred from the still-beating heart of a road kill hedgehog, squashed to death by a Sports Utility Vehicle on a narrow road in Snowdonia.

It's a mad mad world out there, should we choose to let it be so ...

* * *

Broccoli Brassica lived in a village where vegetables were important. By that I don't mean that the mayor and police chief were slightly dull people who needed to get out more, but that Sleepy Backwater on the Mould was a village that celebrated vegetables in the raw with an annual Fruit and Vegetable Competition where rosettes were awarded for Beauty and Taste. It wasn't done in a noisy way. The competition was always contested in a spirit of fair play. In one hundred years only three inhabitants had tried anything devious to win. In 1928 Herbert Flowerdew was publicly disgraced for looking through a telescope at his neighbour's French beans. He never grew again and died that Christmas a broken man.

Quite right too!

In 1953, Marjorie Bastien, the holder of the Cabbage Rosette, became the subject of a police enquiry when a witness thought he'd seen 'a person of the female persuasion' releasing a rabbit into the cabbage patch of her rival, Mrs Thornycroft, on the eve of competition.

Wicked woman!

And in 1993, in the year of the Great Drought, Samuel S. Binnywell was caught feeding his peas individually with a pipette full of imported Italian water!

Off with his head!

It would be fair to say that the vegetable growers of Sleepy Backwater on the Mould were by and large a gentle crowd who cared not a jot who won.

So where Broccoli Brassica came from nobody quite knows, for she was *nothing* like her parents.

She was born into the world shouting, 'My feet are bigger than his over there!' causing the baby in the next cot to not only bawl his eyes out, but to suffer from a lifelong inferiority complex about his tiny feet. An hour later, having refused her mother's breast and demanded a really big bottle instead, she did a huge green poo and insisted that the nurse weigh it for the Record Books.

It soon became clear that size was *everything* to Broccoli. From the moment she got home she demanded bigger rattles, bigger rusks and bigger lumps of bread to feed the ducks with. When she was teething she bit passing dogs with a whoop of 'My teeth are bigger than yours!' And when she was three and had just started playgroup she travelled around in a 4x4 pushchair with bull bars up front.

'I can't reverse!' she shouted when the width of her buggy caused a bottleneck in the school gates. 'You'll have to back up or we'll be stuck here all day!'

From the day she was big enough to pull herself up on a watering can, Broccoli's parents taught her how things were done in Sleepy Backwater on the Mould.

'We like to grow things,' her mother said.

'And sometimes,' her father added, 'if we grow a particularly beautiful vegetable we might enter it into the village show.'

'By beautiful,' interrupted Broccoli, 'I assume you mean big.'

'Not necessarily,' he said.

'No, you *do*!' she screamed, correcting his mistake. 'Because big is beautiful!'

They gave her lessons in growing things: starting with mustard and cress on blotting paper, then broad beans in a jar, then radishes, custard apples, avocadoes and tomatoes. By the time she was four Broccoli, had her own vegetable patch, by the time she was six her vegetables had started to appear in the competition. She won a ninth for a parsnip, a joint seventh for a lovely brace of onions, and a Judge's Commendation (but no rosette) for a beetroot that looked like a fat fairy in the 'Vegetables That Look Like Amusing Objects' section. But it wasn't a first and because it wasn't a first Broccoli wasn't happy. First meant biggest and big was all that Broccoli was interested in.

* * *

For the next two years she pulled out all the stops in an effort to grow the biggest vegetable in the village. She nurtured her plants with lashings of horse manure, round-the-clock sunshine from sun lamps and computerised rainfall from hosepipes installed in the roof of the greenhouse. She constantly expected big things and was always disappointed. Then, when she was eight years old, she dug up a turnip that was big enough to take first prize. Or so she thought. She was so excited that she ran all the way to the village hall.

On the eve of competition competitors always gathered in the village hall for a glass of squash and a muffin so that the vicar, who also doubled up as the judge, could wish them luck and ask for money for the church.

Broccoli burst in late and rushed straight to the front of the room. Her fellow competitors, all of them little old ladies with lilac hair, were shocked to the very soles of their slip-on wellie-boots as she jumped onto a table in front of the vicar and shouted, 'Loooosers! From now on, you old biddies had best stick to jam, because the Vegetable Queen has arrived! My turnip's so big it's going to blow

90

your puny prunes out the water!' It was the first time such an unpleasant display of bad sportsmanship had ever been seen in Sleepy Backwater on the Mould.

'I say,' said the vicar. 'There's no need for that.'

'Oh, don't you start with all your *every man is equal* stuff!' shouted Broccoli. 'The point of a competition is to win and my turnip's the best!'

But pride comes before a fall and the old ladies' shock paled into insignificance alongside the shock that Broccoli was to suffer the following morning.

* * *

That night, while Sleepy Backwater on the Mould closed its eyes to the world, the weevils came. As you may know, weevils are the curse of fruit and vegetable competitions throughout the land, for these little beetles with their flesh-busting jaws *adore* the taste of fruit and vegetables: the bigger the better to suck out the pulp leaving nothing behind but a pile of empty, wrinkled skin. What makes them such a fearsome foe, however, is that they cannot be stopped. They can fly in and feast and nobody knows that they are there. Weevils, you see, are invisible.

INTERESTING FACTS ABOUT NATURE

Number 312 – Invisible Weevils
You've heard the expression, *Hear no weevil,
See no weevil.* It's true. Apparently, weevils fly at
37.64 kilometres per hour; the exact speed at
which the human ear ceases to pick up sounds and
the human eye has a blind spot.

As the church clock struck midnight, the invisible weevils swarmed silently into Sleepy Backwater on the Mould. When their mashing mandibles departed three hours later there was not a fruit or a vegetable left in the village ... except for Broccoli's. Imagine her excitement, therefore, when she awoke. No matter that every other grower was distraught and old ladies had collapsed on their artichoke beds and were watering the stalks with their tears, Broccoli whooped for joy and ran down to the village hall with her produce in a bag.

'You want me to judge them?!' gasped the vicar incredulously. 'After all that went on last night?'

'Yes,' said Broccoli. 'I want to win.'

'But people are grieving,' he said.

'For fruit and vegetables!' sneered Broccoli. 'Get a life! Look, if nobody else has got anything to enter mine *must* be the biggest, therefore I win! Just get on with it.'

'Size isn't everything,' said the vicar, tipping Broccoli's fruit and vegetables onto the table. But in this case it *was*. 'I'm afraid they're all too small,' he said. 'I can't award them any prizes.'

'Too small!' she yelled. 'What about the turnip?'

'Even the turnip. They're all below regulation size. That's why the weevils left them. Now if you'll excuse me this year's contest is cancelled.'

Then the vicar rose from his seat, popped a straw hat on his head and left the building. It was at that moment, as the cold blade of disappointment cleaved her heart in two, that Broccoli decided she'd had it with fair play. Water, sunshine and steaming manure were for losers. This time next year she was going to win *no matter what*!

* * *

She spent the winter in the library, reading. When she emerged in the spring, three months before competition day, she had worked out a foolproof plan. To grow the biggest fruit and vegetables in the village she would need to master the art of genetic modification.

The first time genetic modification (GM) was ever used in Britain was when they made GMTV (a light-weight breakfast television programme) by combining the genes from a stick of candyfloss with the genes from a minor-celebrity's hat.

Broccoli had a busy few days. Having planted her seeds as normal she went out and bought the largest vegetable she could find, which happened to be a pumpkin. She then trotted along to her local science supplies shop for a syringe, a pipette, a petri dish and a bottle of growth hormone. Back at home, she sucked some big cells out of the pumpkin, mixed them up with the growth hormone in the Petri dish and injected the solution through the skin of each fruit and vegetable on her patch.

'Well, that was simple,' she said when the last gooseberry had been genetically modified. 'I can't think why scientists make such a fuss!'

Her parents were horrified when Broccoli told

them what she had done.

'But you can't tamper with Nature,' gasped her mother. 'It's cheating!'

'Why should anyone know,' said Broccoli coldly, 'unless *you* tell them?'

'*Somebody* will know,' said her father, looking up from the basket he was weaving.

'Who?' she asked.

'The weevils,' he whispered. Anyone who'd been brought up in Sleepy Backwater on the Mould, as her father had, knew the weevils inside out. 'They always go for biggest crops first. If your cheaty-ones are half as big as you say they'll be, the weevils will eat them first.'

'Ah ha!' she whooped triumphantly. 'That's why I've planted them all in the greenhouse. Weevils may be clever, but they can't fly through glass.'

'That depends,' he said mysteriously.

'On what?'

'On how big they are.'

Broccoli didn't realise that weevils came in different sizes. 'You mean not all weevils are the size of flying ants?'

'Not all flying ants are the size of flying ants,' he replied mysteriously. 'Not any more.'

There was only six weeks to go until the Fruit and Vegetable competition. Every other competitor in the village had been lovingly tending their produce for months, but Broccoli was in no rush. She knew that *her* fruit and veg could grow in the jiggle of a gene. And she was right. One week after planting out, her carrots were three feet long, her tomatoes were as big as beach balls and her raspberries were the size of bowler hats. Neighbours stared over the garden wall in envy and the talk in the pub was that she had inflated them all with a bicycle pump. She  got so cocky that she weeded out the smaller fruits and vegetables and threw them on the compost heap, so that there was more room for the bigger plants to grow.

Occasionally, she got an odd crop on a plant,

where she had obviously *over*-modified its genes and mutations had occurred. There was a Breadfruit Tree growing croissants and soft baps; an Eggplant that was growing a Full English Cooked Breakfast – sausages off one stem, fried eggs off another, bacon and mushrooms off two more; a Cauliflower plant  that had produced a Collie Dog with a flower instead of a tail; and a Tomato plant that defied belief. It was growing tinned tomatoes; that is to say, tomatoes *already in a tin*! The tin grew with the fruit! Broccoli took sensible precautions with these freaks of Nature. To avoid cross contamination she tucked them away on a top shelf in the greenhouse; all except for the Collie dog, which she picked and kept as a pet.

And a very good pet it made as well, because it spoke fluent English.

Then, one week before Competition Day, just as her father had predicted, the weevils returned. They caught a whiff of Broccoli's big-boys and slipped into the greenhouse in the middle of the night like moon-shadows. They gorged themselves sick on her outsized crop and flew home without touching another stalk or stem in the village. Broccoli's fruit and vegetables were so big that the weevils couldn't fit another morsel in!

In the morning, when Broccoli ran into the garden to check on her prize winners, it looked like a bomb had exploded. The grass was covered in the wrinkled skins of aubergines, melons, peppers, courgettes, cucumbers and peaches and the aluminium frame of the greenhouse had been snapped into a hundred twisted pieces.

'How could teeny-tiny beetles do this?' howled Broccoli through a waterfall of tears. Her father gestured towards the compost heap.

'Have you ever put any plants on there?' he asked.

'Only the weediest ones.'

'Weedy they might have been,' he said, 'but they were still genetically modified.'

'They got in,' her mother explained, 'because they ate what you threw away.'

'You mean the weevils ate the growth hormone in my fruit and veg . . . and grew?'

'That's right. They didn't have to fly through the glass to get in. They opened the door by stamping on the roof!'

'That *is* big,' gasped Broccoli.

'Very big,' shuddered her mother. 'I was woken by a loud chomping, so I opened the curtain to see what was causing it and there they were, silhouetted against the moon, drooling and oozing. They were hideous.'

'You mean you saw them and didn't stop them!' shrieked Broccoli.

'How could I? They were the size of Shire horses!'

'I think *now*, is probably a very good time to stop meddling with Nature, don't you?' said Mr Brassica. Clearly Broccoli did *not*, because just then the Collie dog rushed into the room wagging its flower.

'You're never going to believe what I've just found,' it said, holding up a tinned tomato plant. 'This is what the weevils left. They couldn't eat it.'

'Are you saying what I think you're saying?' grinned Broccoli.

'I think so,' said the mutant dog. 'I'm pointing out that the weevils might be big, but they obviously can't cut through metal!' Broccoli danced with excitement.

'If I want to win the competition,' she cried, 'I'm going to have to grow my vegetables in tins!' Her nervous father begged her not to do it.

'If the weevils have mutated *once* to get food,' he

said, 'what is to stop them from mutating again?'
But Broccoli was beyond reason.

'You know what your trouble is?' she sneered.
'You *think* too much, daddy. This isn't science
fiction. This is the *real* world!'

* * *

And so it was, with one week to go before the vicar
judged the Sleepy Backwater on the Mould Fruit
and Vegetable competition, that Broccoli spent the
night extracting the genetic material from the
tinned tomato plant. Dawn was breaking as she
mixed the genetic sample with the growth
hormone and injected the solution into a tray of
new seedlings. Then she cleared a patch in the
garden, dug lots of holes and planted the seedlings
out.

'Don't forget the electric fence,' Cauliflower
reminded her.

'You are a good dog,' she smiled. 'What would I
do without you?' An hour later, Broccoli switched
the fence on. 'There,' she said smugly.
'That should keep the giant weevils
out!' Then she wished her
genetically modified plants
'Happy Growing!' and went

indoors to dream of victory.

Such a shame she didn't check what was buried in the ground first . . .

* * *

There is a good reason why weevils cannot be seen or heard when they fly and it has nothing to do with a cruising speed of 37.64 kilometres per hour. They don't fly. They have wings, but they don't work. They flap them to fool gardeners into thinking that they *can* fly, but they can't. They live underground, so that while all eyes are looking up at the sky for an attack, they can cunningly sneak up on their food from *below*. It turns out that the lie about weevils being invisible was originally leaked to the press by the weevils themselves. It suited them to keep humans in the dark.

So, by moving her plants out of the greenhouse, which had been built on a concrete base, Broccoli had played right into the weevils' mandibles!

For two days she watched her patch and waited. Then suddenly at 10.15 on the morning of Day 3, her Mark II genetically-modified fruit and vegetable plants started to grow! By lunchtime her patch was glinting with thousands of shiny tins full of fruit and vegetables. There were so many in fact, that she didn't notice when one or two went missing; when twenty tins of Brussels sprouts, a dozen tins of pineapple, thirty tins of asparagus and a tinned Savoy cabbage disappeared into the ground, where greedy flesh-busting jaws consumed them, genetic mutations and all!

Come the night before the competition, Broccoli sat in her bedroom window and admired her bumper crop.

'Look at that,' she said proudly to her cauliflower. 'Those tins are big! Why anyone bothers to grow stuff normally beats me. Tins are the future, you know. They keep the weevils out.'

'You're right,' said the dog. 'Some people are scared of genetically modified crops, but I think there's a lot to be said for them.'

'Yes, you would,' laughed Broccoli. 'After all, you were a vegetable once too!' Then she took herself off to bed and dreamed of rosettes and victory.

On the stroke of midnight, the ground stirred under Broccoli's patch. It quivered as if telegraphing an earthquake. Ripples of loose dirt shot out across the garden and peppered the walls of the house. Suddenly, there was a loud groan, the ground fell away and a huge hole opened up inside the electric fence.

Out of this hole poked a pair of wiry feelers. They twitched like bullwhips as they 'sniffed' for danger, then the first of the giant weevils crawled out. The moon reflected off its shiny black shell as its fat legs scrabbled to get a footing in the soil. A second armoured snout nudged the first weevil from behind and the monstrous bug popped out of the ground. It had mutated again. Having eaten the genetically modified cans of fruit and vegetables the weevil had grown a kitchen accessory. Protruding from the centre of its forehead, jutting out like a long flat horn, was a huge silver can opener, which it whizzed around the edge of a tin until the lid dropped off. Then it thrust its great elephantine snout into the tin and sucked up the fruity flesh inside. Emboldened by their scout's success, hundreds more weevils burst out of the hole and set to work with their tin openers.

The sound of metallic crunching penetrated Broccoli's dream. She woke with a start and leaped from her bed. She pulled back her curtains and gasped.

'No!' she cried. 'No!' Her vegetable patch was a

riot of giant mutant can-opening weevils. The electric fence had been crushed by the weight of numbers as they squirmed out of the earth like the Devil's spawn. Their mandibles munched as they devoured her prize winning produce! 'Stop!' she yelled, banging on the window. 'Stop! I've got a can of insecticide and I'm not afraid to use it!'

She lost her mind. She ran downstairs and rushed into the garden, spraying a path through the long black legs with her can of 'BUG OFF!' She tried to scare the mutant weevils away by pulling fierce faces and screaming, but they were ten times her size, with only one thing on their teeny tiny insect minds. Food.

When the weevil attached its can opener to the top of Broccoli's head she felt only a small nick. But when it started turning her around and the blade carved through her skull she felt like her brains were boiling, and fainted. And in that comatose state the weevil removed the top of her head and sucked out the flesh and bones from her body, leaving nothing on the ground, but a pile of empty, wrinkled skin for her parents to find in the morning.

But that was not the end of it. Two days later, Broccoli Brassica was genetically re-modified herself; from human being to weevil dung!

Well, her flesh and bones were. The rest of her came down to me a scrawny, pallid pile of wrinkled skin. WHAT A TRAGIC WASTE . . . of her room, I mean. Knowing how much she liked BIG things, I'd spent literally HOURS filling that broom cupboard with old boxes to make it so TINY that she'd be REALLY REALLY miserable, then she goes and loses her body! Selfish, selfish, SELFISH girl!

Nowadays she lives in a plastic bag that I hang on the back of the Hoover cupboard door. After all that trouble she put me through to get her room just right it's the least I can do.

I make sure she pays her way now  too. I popped a party hat on her head to cover the bit where the weevils opened her up and put a zip down her side, and now I use her for all manner of chamber chores — pyjama case, dirty linen bag, duster. I did try her out as a hot water bottle cover, but the guest found it a bit spooky going to bed with a dead body, even though it was warm. I had to really FORCE them!

P.S. For those of you who are interested. Mrs Popplethwaite won the Sleepy Backwater on the Mould Fruit and Vegetable competition with what the vicar described as 'the most succulent gooseberries I have ever tasted.' Well done, Mrs Popplethwaite.

Does anyone know what the time is?

Yes. Tom. It's time to say goodbye!

Right. Of all the freaks of Nature. this next story is the freakiest I know. Not because the boy is a freak but because Nature is. This sort of natural disaster happens only once in a universe. which is why I've left it till last. As you will soon see there can be no stories after this one.

THE END IS NIGH

TOM TIME

Some children are like meerkats. They are up and buzzing, always looking around for the next thing to do, alert, energetic and connected to the world so as to get the most out of it. Others are like slugs. Maybe they have thicker skulls than the rest of us, or their brains are wrapped in greaseproof paper. Whatever it is, the outside world takes longer to get through, so reaction time is slower.

In Tom's case, he was always one hour behind the rest of the world. If he was told to be somewhere at nine, he got there for ten. This was partly because he was so disorganised, but mainly because the effort required to be on time was simply too much for his sleepy body to bear. This meant that every single morning he was late for school.

'One hour late *again*, Tom!' His form teacher's angry eye twitched like a humming bird's wings.

'No I'm not,' protested Tom, pointing to his watch. 'My watch says—'

His watch said ten o'clock. 'Oh yeah. How did that happen?' Twitch twitch!

He was always late for lunch.

'Sorry, love,' said the dinner lady. 'Closed!'

'What is it with lunch in this school?' moaned Tom. 'I miss it every day.'

'You need to come an hour earlier,' she said.

'But it's only ten past one—' He caught sight of his watch and paused. 'Oh. It's ten past two.'

'Exactly,' she said. 'And lunch finishes at ten past one. Why do you think the rest of your classmates are doing gymnastics in the dining hall?'

Tom had wondered why there were twenty children locked in a shaky human pyramid on the very spot where the tables should have been.

'Um, excuse me,' he said to the gym teacher. 'Do you know that there's somebody missing from that pyramid? There's a hole in the bottom row.'

'I wonder who should be there?' she said sarcastically.

'It's not *me* is it?' said Tom. 'Is it me who's meant to be standing in that hole?'

'Yes,' she said as the pyramid collapsed. 'Bit late now, though.'

* * *

Tom was one hour late for everything; buses, swimming, TV programmes, handing in homework, scoring goals . . .

'I just scored *seven*!' he yelled, bursting into the locker room after the match only to find the rest of his team mates changed and ready to go back to school on the coach.

'The match finished an hour ago,' they said.

'Oh, right.' Tom scratched his head. 'I thought the opposition weren't putting up much of a fight.'

Tom's mother maintained that Tom had the laidback brain of a three-toed sloth. Apparently, or so her story goes, Tom was three when his brain accidentally fell out after a sneezing fit at the zoo. It had rolled past the monkey cage, through the bars of the three-toed sloth enclosure and had stopped next to a nursing mummy sloth with her baby. Alert to the medical dangers of her son not having a brain, Tom's mother had wasted no time in reaching through the bars, picking up her son's brain and squeezing it back inside his head. In her haste, however, she had picked up the wrong object. The next thing Tom knew, mummy sloth was cuddling a squidgy, pink cauliflower containing all of Tom's knowledge, while Tom had a small, hairy, brain that was lazy, yawned and scratched its bum.

Which explains why he used to love watching TV programmes about sloths. He'd hold out his arms to the television and cry, 'Mama!'

Basically, Tom was one hour late for life, because being *on* time was too much like hard work. And being late gave him more time to sleep. Having a lie-in was what made him late for school every morning, which in turn made him late *leaving* school, which in turn made him miss the bus home, which in turn made him walk, which meant that he never got home before seven o'clock, by which time he was exhausted and could do no more than start the whole vicious cycle again.

'Just going to my bedroom for a lie down,' he'd announce, as he stumbled through the front door, dropped his satchel on the floor and climbed the stairs.

'Supper's in five minutes,' his mother would reply.

'I'll be there,' he'd shout back as he reached the landing. But he never was. Or at least he *was* there, but one hour late. So that when he walked into the kitchen, supper was always cleared up, and his parents were always watching telly in the sitting room.

* * *

On this one particular evening, having missed out on spaghetti bolognese, Tom shuffled into the sitting room and leant against the door frame.

'Hello, Mum. Hello, Dad,' he said sheepishly. 'When's supper?'

'Tomorrow, Tom. We ate tonight's an hour ago.'

'Oh.' His mother never minced her words. 'Right,' said Tom. 'Just going to my bedroom for a lie down then.'

As Tom turned towards the stairs, his shovel-faced father piped up with, 'Maybe the lad needs to take up boxing.' Tom's father had been a boxer for more years than he could remember, which explained the broken nose, the marshmallow brain and the voice like a slowed-down record. 'That's all about good timing – boxing.' He threw a few air-punches and ducked out the way of an imaginary right hook. 'Ding-ding. Seconds out!'

'Maybe you should have a lie down too,' said

Tom's mother, patting her husband on his bald head.

'Yes. Maybe I should,' he replied. 'I could do with one. Ding-ding. Lights out!' But before he could close his eyes, Tom's mother sat forward on the sofa and pointed at the corner of the room.

'Wait!' she cried. Tom stopped in the hallway and turned to see what she was shouting about. 'Look at the news on the telly!'

The newsreader looked serious. 'Scientists have just released the following warning,' she said grimly, turning to watch the report on her monitor. The picture cut to three frightened scientists in white coats standing in front of a bank of microphones.

'Don't just stand there!' one of them screamed at the camera. 'Can't you see? We're all going to die! We're all going to die! Aaaaaaaaaaaaaaaa aaaaaaaaaaaaaaaagh!' Then all three scientists ran around the studio flapping their arms like chickens, removing their clothes and pulling out their hair. The newsreader looked confused when the director cut back to her.

'I'm sorry. We seem to have the wrong report there. Let's go live instead to the Senior

Government Spokesman for National Disasters.' The picture changed again, only this time to the Home Office in Westminster, where the Senior Government Spokesman, wearing a sober blue suit and fully-prepared frown, steadied himself to address the world's press.

Suddenly, he burst into tears. 'Don't just stand there!' he hollered. 'Can't you see? We're all going to die! We're all going to die! Aaaaaaaaaaaaaaa aaaaaaaaaaaaaaaaaagh!' Then he ran round the room waving his arms like a cowardly bear being chased by a swarm of bees. This time when the picture cut back to the newsreader she looked fed up.

'Right, so it's left to muggins here to tell you,' she said, adjusting the papers on the desk in front of her. 'At midday tomorrow the world is going to end. Mother Nature's had enough of us, apparently. She's fed up with the way we mistreat her planet and wants us out. So she's organised for a big explosion in the centre of the earth that will probably sound something like this: *Kaboom!* After that, who knows? Blotto, probably. Anyway, space shuttles will be leaving for the Moon at eleven am. There's room on board for every human being and every animal on the planet. Don't be late. That is the end of this Ne—' Tom's mother switched the newsreader off with the remote control and sat there looking stunned.

'Gosh!' gasped Tom's father. 'The end of the world. Ding–ding. Last round.'

'Did you hear what she said, Tom? Don't be late.'

'For what?' Tom had returned to his leaning position in the doorway.

'Weren't you listening?' sighed his mother.

'I was having a little snooze,' said Tom with a weak smile.

'Then listen *now!*' she barked.

'Tomorrow morning we have to be on a Space Shuttle by eleven o'clock sharp or it will leave for the moon without us!' Knowing Tom the way she did, that was going to be easier said than done.

To compensate for Tom's habitual lateness, it was decided that he should get up one hour earlier. So his mum reset every alarm clock in the house, rigged the car horn, overrode the lighting circuit, pre-set the television, radio and stereo to come on automatically, fed the birds with Early Bird Worm biscuits, hired a small brass band and a cannon, and phoned Number 10 Downing Street to organise for Concorde to be taken out of mothballs and flown past the house at six o'clock precisely. Then she went to bed.

* * *

The following morning at six o'clock precisely pandemonium erupted. Alarm bells **rang**, the car horn wailed, the house lights **flashed**, the TV, radio and stereo **blasted** out three different rock songs at full volume, the songbirds **sang**, the Colliery Brass Band on the front lawn **played** 'And Now The End Is Near', a cannon from the gun deck of Nelson's *Victory* **fired** a volley of explosive charges and Concorde flew overhead **bursting** the clouds with its sonic boom. This was enough noise to not only **wake** the dead but get them up to **complain** to the authorities as well.

But Tom slept right through.

He woke up an hour late to find his bedroom upside down.

'Have I slept through a hurricane?' he yawned, sitting up and rubbing his eyes. His mother had a large, open suitcase partially packed at her feet. Strewn across the floor and bursting out of every drawer and cupboard were all of Tom's clothes.

'We're leaving for the moon today. I'm trying to pack,' she said tersely.

'The moon,' he said vacantly. 'We're going to the moon?'

'Don't you remember anything?' she snapped.

'You're my mum,' he said flatly.

'It's the end of the world!'

'Oh come on, it's not that bad. I mean you can be a bit naggy, but most of the time you're all right.'

'*No!* Today is the end of the world!' Tom's mother was clearly teetering on the edge of a breakdown, but Tom didn't notice.

'Oh yeah,' he said turning over in his bed. 'Don't have to get up for a bit then.' But he *did* have to get up. She pulled the duvet off his body and threw it on the floor. 'The shuttle leaves in two hours!' she shouted.

'And it won't wait,' added Tom's father, as he wandered past the door carrying a box of boxing paraphernalia. 'Ding-ding. All aboard please.'

Now, you would have thought that the imminent explosion of the planet might have sharpened Tom's mind, but his lovely warm duvet dulled it. Having dragged it back off the floor, he curled up underneath it again and drifted back into blissful half-sleep. From that moment on, it didn't matter how urgently Tom's parents called him, Tom was always going to be one hour behind.

08.00 am

'Breakfast is on the table!' yelled his mother.

'Just getting up,' came Tom's reply, as he slipped out of bed.

09.00 am

'Time to finish packing!' she hollered from the hall.

'Just brushing my teeth,' mumbled Tom with a mouthful of toothpaste.

09.45 am

'Taxi's here for the shuttle!' screamed his mother and father together.

'Just getting dressed,' replied Tom, as he looked at the clothes his mother had left him and chose a different shirt.

09.57 am

'Taxi *still* here for shuttle!' Tom's parents' voices were high–pitched and squeaky, as Tom descended the stairs at a leisurely pace.

'All right, keep you hair on,' he said. 'I'm here now, aren't I?'

'Thank goodness,' said his mother. 'I really thought you weren't going to make it.'

'Don't be silly,' chuckled Tom, turning towards the kitchen. 'Just got to have breakfast first.'

'There's no time for breakfast!' she shrieked, stopping him in his tracks.

'But you always said that breakfast was the most important meal of the day.'

'Not when there's a taxi waiting,' she said.

'And this is the most important day in the history of the human race so breakfast must be more important than ever today.'

'I don't have time for an argument, Tom. The taxi has other people to take to the shuttle.'

'It's not my fault if it's early.'

A blood vessel burst on the tip of his mother's nose.

'IT'S NOT EARLY! YOU'RE AN HOUR LATE!'

'But I'm hungry,' complained Tom, as she took a deep breath and counted to ten.

'Then you should have got up in time for breakfast.'

'No. I'm hungry, because my mean mother didn't cook me supper last night.'

'Because you were an hour late coming to the table!'

'Ding-ding.' Tom's father brought news from the street. 'The cab driver says he can't wait. Either we go now, or we don't go at all.'

'We're coming!' growled Tom's mother, but when she turned around to drag Tom outside, Tom had disappeared. She found him in the kitchen putting a slice of bread in the toaster.

'Can I bring my toast?'

'*No!*' she cried, an inch away from tears. '*Leave* the toast, Tom. The toast doesn't matter. If we don't leave right this instant we'll BE toast! The world is about to explode!'

'But I've got the bread out the packet now,' he said. 'Seems a waste.'

'Right! That's it! I'm going. You can make your own way to the moon!'

And with that, Tom's mother turned on her heels and marched out of the house, slamming the door behind her. For the first time that morning, Tom looked worried.

'Hang on. Mum! *Mum!* Wait! *Mum!*'

10.03 am

Tom ran out of the house with a piece of toast in his hand, expecting to find his parents gone, but they were still sitting in the cab waiting for him. The driver had the engine running.

'Oh, you're still here,' said Tom.

'Of course we're still here,' growled his mother.

'I really thought you'd gone without me,' he said.

She took a deep breath and controlled her temper just long enough to say, 'Well, we didn't. Now get into the car, Tom.' But Tom had something on his mind.

'There's just one thing I need to know first,' he said.

It was the cab driver who exploded with incandescent rage, bursting out of his seat and yelling at Tom across the roof of the car. 'WHAT? WHAT IS IT NOW, YOU STUPID BOY?'

Tom smiled to make the cab driver like him. 'Where's the marmalade?' he asked. The cab driver jumped back into the car, gunned the gas and disappeared up the street in a cloud of black smoke.

'What?' coughed Tom. 'What? What did I say?'

* * *

That was that. Tom was on his own, and had less than an hour to get himself to the space shuttle. So he finished his breakfast, read a comic on the loo, played a game of Alien Apocalypse on his Gamebox, changed his socks, gelled his hair, squeezed a spot, pumped up the tyres on his bicycle, had a little think about the end of the world, left a note on the kitchen table for Mother Nature . . .

SORRY WE'VE MESSED UP THE PLANET, MRS NATURE!

. . . and left for the shuttle with fifteen seconds to spare.

10.59 am

Tom cycled as fast as he could to reach the

shuttle-port, but it was not fast enough. The space shuttle blasted off exactly one hour before he arrived at the launch site.

11.59 am

Tom arrived at the launch site. The only human being left on earth, he stood at the gates and stared at the scorched concrete underneath the empty launch pad.

He was late again.
Not for the end of the world though. He was on time for that!

12.00 pm

At 12.00 pm precisely, the world exploded and ceased to exist.

Bizarrely Tom survived. He was trapped in a bubble of Tom Time that allowed him to float through Space for exactly fifty-nine minutes and fifty-nine seconds, when, precisely one hour later than the rest of the world, Tom exploded, and his atoms were scattered to the fourteen corners of the universe.

THE END (literally)

I know what you're thinking. You're thinking. 'How come if the world has ended I'm still sitting here reading this book?' How do you think? Have you paid NO attention while I've been telling you this tale? Tom Time kept him safe for one hour. YOU must be trapped in a time bubble too. Think about it! It makes complete sense. You are a child. are you not. therefore you are sluggardly. You are a moaning. self-centred whinger who won't do anything at anyone's pace but your OWN. Of course you're trapped in a time bubble. All Stink-fishes are! But now is the time to WAKE UP!!

I don't want to start a panic or anything. but the world is going to blow up at any moment. It's true! Why would I lie about something so serious? Pack your bags this instant and get out NOW!

This is a list of what you will need to pack for the end of the world:

Antiseptic cream and plasters (for bumps and bruises)

Ray gun to kill aliens (optional)

Trainers (six pairs not optional)

Toothbrush

There is only one place you can go to be safe.

123

And it's not the moon. The moon is made out of cheese and is prone to attack from Space Mice. You do not want to be attacked by them. It's a long, lingering death. They'll break into your space ship and nibble your ration packs from underneath, working their way up to the top. So from above the packet will still look full. For thirty years you won't notice that anything's missing. Then suddenly, one day, all your rations will be gone. And then you'll starve to death and the Space Mice will steal your ship.

Honest! It's not a word of a lie!

The only place you'll be entirely safe is down here in The Darkness. I know you think I'm evil and only want you down here so I can have fun at your expense with a little light torture, but not every day will be like that! Some days, we'll open all the windows and let the sun shine in . . . actually, maybe not. If the world has ended there won't be any sun left. We'll do finger-painting and drawing with yoghurt pots and pasta. I'll teach you how to play the tambourine and we'll listen to music on the gramophone . . . WELL, I DON'T KNOW! You tell me what children do for entertainment nowadays?!

Look. I'm not pretending that I don't have a teeny-tiny temper or that I can replace your parents (although I have got loads of money and am always looking for crazy ways to get rid of it). but we've got enough jam doughnuts in the cellars to last for months and Broccoti can grow us some of her tinned tomatoes. It'll be fun.

Besides. your room's ready. I've even installed double glazing so that ~~nobody will hear you scream~~ you won't hear the bang when the world explodes! Go on. Be a sport. I've got you a ticket.

🚂 Brutish Rail ☠ Brutish Rail 🚂

THE DISORIENT EXPRESS
KING'S CROSS TO
THE HOTHELL DARKNESS
(Please Note: This is the end of the line)

ONE WAY TICKET

Reserved: Ball & Chain C16
There is no buffet car on this train. If you do not bring your own sandwiches you will have to eat your own feet.

Price: Your Soul   *Slave Class*

Shall I expect you?

Where are you going? Don't walk away from me when I'm talking to you. I thought we had a deal.

All right. I lied about the end of the world. I admit it was a fib to get you down here. But I'm so lonely.

Take pity on an old man.

I'M RUNNING OUT OF BRIQUETTES!

THE
END
IS
HERE